MW01045983

Guts and Glory...
An American Story....
You GOT's to be CRAZY!!"

Guts and Glory...
An American Story....
You GOT's to be CRAZY!!"

You've GOT to Be Crazy! The Webb-Based
Science to Twenty-Second-Century Sales Success

The first minority and executive to lead a global sales force
by inspiring people around the world for the Kirby Company

ARTIS WEBB

Library of Congress Control Number:		2014916484
ISBN:	Hardcover	978-1-4990-7272-3
	Softcover	978-1-4990-7274-7
	eBook	978-1-4990-7276-1

This book was printed in the United States of America.

Rev. date: 09/15/2014

To order additional copies of this book, contact:
Xlibris LLC
1-888-795-4274
www.Xlibris.com
Orders@Xlibris.com
659217

CONTENTS

FOREWORD

Some people believe the Kirby Company is an abnormal and CRAZY route to pursue a career opportunity. However, Mr. Windfeldt learned early in his career that *what is normal IS NOT the normal route to success.* Mr. Gene Windfeldt formerly served as the president and chief executive officer of the Kirby Company. He arrived from a humble background. His father served in World War II while his mother worked hard to keep things together. Mr. Windfeldt arrived at Kirby with over ten years of corporate experience under his belt. Therefore, while attending the University of Minnesota in 1964, Mr. Windfeldt started his career as a part-time dealer at the Kirby Company, a subsidiary of the Scott Fetzer Company owned by Warren Buffett's Berkshire Hathaway. He became a distributor in 1968 and developed the largest Kirby distributorship, exceeding one thousand units per month. In 1982, he became a divisional supervisor in Kirby. Mr. Windfeldt developed the highest market penetration in the company and ultimately became president and CEO for the Kirby Company during the years of 1988–1997. Thus, he applied this hard-work ethic to Kirby and quickly figured out the business. Mr. Windfeldt wanted to help other people achieve the same success as evidenced by his intentional investment in Artis Webb.

In 1982, Mr. Windfeldt met Artis Webb. Both traveled on the same incentive trips. Mr. Windfeldt maintains a special passion for keeping a mental inventory of people with high potential. Therefore, he followed the progression of Artis's successes within the organization. Following an unexpected accident, Artis ran into hard times. As a successful distributor, business is contingent upon the distributor's attitude, example, and confidence. Mr. Windfeldt reached out to Artis to see if he would be interested in serving as national sales manager. In 1992, Artis eagerly accepted the role of national sales manager, and his career took off again!

Gene shared, "Artis is a good individual who is gifted in his ability to execute the job. In fact, Artis probably didn't know he had this talent to become national sales manager." Mr. Windfeldt was honored to give him the opportunity to create success within this new executive role. As national sales manager, Artis traveled across the country as a successful executive for the Kirby Company.

Later, within other roles, he would travel around the globe and receive the same reception from over seventy countries as received in the United States. Thus, Artis became a legend gifted in his ability to communicate and motivate people, resulting in his becoming a leader larger than life. Artis is a talented encourager, always full of positive energy, a skilled deliverer of outstanding speeches to Kirby people, and bountiful in sharing his business skills.

Mr. Windfeldt boasted, "Artis is one of the people I am most proud of. He is not only good in the business, but equally rich in family." As mentioned, prior to Artis's start in Kirby, he could only find jobs that paid $2.69 per hour, or minimum wage. He knew right from the beginning this salary would not provide the type of foundation, vision, and foundational support desired for his family. Mr. Windfeldt confirmed that most leaders in Kirby came from the same struggle. The family is the *why* of what you are working for. Most adults never experience an opportunity to build a succession plan for a family business. Thus, it was very gratifying and fulfilling to work with Artis and watch him evolve as a business leader through the maturation process.

In 1997, Mr. Windfeldt departed from the Kirby Company as an owner of Preferred Credit Inc. (a company he founded and kept with the Kirby Company's knowledge). This nationwide provider of financing is dedicated to the special needs of the direct-sales industry. The company now exceeds 100 million dollars in size with over 250 employees. As the Kirby Company is one of the largest direct-selling organizations in the world, Mr. Windfeldt applied many of the same nurtured skills and people principles he gained in the Kirby Company. For example: (a) invest energy into developing people; (b) maintain an open-door policy; (c) if a better opportunity comes along, be willing to help sales leaders get the next job. For example, Mr. Windfeldt provided résumé support, letters of recommendations, and positive acknowledgment of contributions to the company. When potential employees see Preferred Credit Inc., they know they have a winner.

Thus, Mr. Windfeldt has created another success with Preferred Credit Inc. with 250-plus employees across the United States and Great Britain, building legacy for families. Artis admired Mr. Windfeldt and appreciated the time and leadership that he invested in his career. Artis is now working to create an enterprise and environment where sales leaders, his family, and future sales leaders of Kirby can thrive. During the closing of this interview, Mr. Windfeldt shared that regardless of the role held by Artis, "he continued to shine that positive input on other people, a perfect example of what you can do in life. . . . When one can create that type of impact on people, *it is truly life changing!*"

Changing History and Growing with Diversity

Artis was the first African American to rise to an executive level in the Kirby Company. In a short period, Artis evolved to the one of the top representations, promoting distributors, distributor entrepreneurs, outreach distributor, and national sales managers in the business. Artis traveled to seventy-plus countries, shared salutations of several languages, and always left a positive image wherever he traveled. His leadership example changed lives. Appreciation for hard work is the heart and soul of the Kirby business. Rewards such as social proof, parties, recognition, trophies, travel—including thirteen-day tours around the world—are provided to demonstrate what a sales team can EXPECT by building a successful career in Kirby. Artis is a wonderful example of a person who succeeds in this business. Today we can see the fulfillment and results of his successful business and career. Kirby's current president was also inspired by the incredible leadership of Artis Webb.

Bud Miley, Current President of World Wide Field Sales for the Kirby Company

There I was at 23 years of age as I watched 'Artis Webb'
someone bigger than life walking by. He invited me
to sit down at the pool deck.

—*Mr. Bud Miley*

Mr. Miley's growing years were invested watching his father (who worked for Frank Venditti) travel around the New York and England areas helping Distributors in the Kirby Company. Therefore, it was no surprise for Mr. Miley to express an interest in Kirby during the summers. He heard about Kirby's scholarship programs to help college costs. Therefore, during summer breaks he tried it. The outcome resulted in sales, increased self-confidence, and the desire to take one semester off. Thereafter, his career in Kirby evolved from selling Kirby's as a dealer, team leader, distributor trainee 1987, and today President of World Wide Field Sales for the Kirby Company. Thus, Mr. Miley's success as a frontline contributor to dealer evolved over a period of 30+ years.

During his early years in Kirby, his life intersected with Artis Webb. In 1987, Artis was an Outreached Distributor for the Kirby Company. Mr. Miley became a Distributor in 1989. Artis and Mr. Miley met on various trips. He remembers Artis' talent for sharing good advice. Miley shares: "There I was at 23 years of age as I watched 'Artis Webb' someone bigger than life walking by. He invited me to sit down at the pool deck!" This is how we met. Artis has a special talent for making people feel important. He even promised to come visit me one day.

A year later, he kept his promise and arrived to my home while I served as a Distributor.

When Artis called, it was really special.

— *Mr. Bud Miley*

Working in Kirby, time can move very fast. Life happens so fast, you are working on a 30-day window, after you hit one goal and have another 30-day goal. As Artis was the National Sales Manager, he was charged to travel all over the world. Yet he was never too busy to serve as one of Mr. Miley's mentors. Mr. Miley shared: "When Artis called, it was really special." He took time to run his sales meeting with quality. Artis had a celebrity reputation! Kirby is a great company in the sense that you are in business for yourself, but not alone by yourself. Sales forces will receive no end of Divisional Supervisor support, create a wealth of camaraderie, and explore opportunities to apply your talents. The Kirby structure is a perfect match for the new generation. This group is the most entrepreneurial generation I have seen. Today young people want to own their own business. Kirby is a place where *any generation* can enjoy fun, receive value for their talents, have a great opportunity to become successful, and build a great life!

Artis has consistently been one of the top Distributors. He can become the top Distributor in the world. Leon Thomas, the current *No. 1* Distributor in the world started with Artis. I am confident that Artis will continue to give, promote, and share the opportunity. I am inspired to show up every day because I enjoy the fun, conversations with Kirby people, engage fun experiences in various positions, challenge, and competition.

ACKNOWLEDGMENTS

The purpose behind CRAZY is to recognize that it takes guts to succeed in life. When the glory can be validated, it can become an American story. The guts to success is the intestinal fortitude to apply your natural-born talents, push yourself forward, and develop the mind-set, mental toughness, and mental competence to *pursue your dreams*. This is how you become impregnated with the glory to deliver this story. When you buy into this vision, onlookers will say, "You've got to be CRAZY!" At least until the manifestation of your lifework validates itself.

Over twenty years ago, I started mentally writing this book. My words arrived from a lifetime of research, experience, study, teaching, learning, leadership, and self-improvement through increased understanding of many great mentors. To my surprise, after discussing this with a few good friends, I am honored to share my forty years of experience and application of various lessons into a self-help book. Arriving to this finish is comparable to climbing Mount Everest, figuratively speaking. Although this is one of the most challenging and highest mountains to climb, I accomplished this feat by supporting the floodgates of my belief required to achieve any goal. I believe this component is necessary. All things are possible for he that believes.

Before sharing the CRAZY story, I am compelled to thank my passionate team of mentors, entrepreneurs, family, and friends for their commitment in working with me to bring this project home. In the past, I experienced how seemingly ordinary people used their influence to do extraordinary things and make a powerful impact on others' lives. Therefore, this is my opportunity to thank the special people who made a positive impact on my life.

David Stewart is a very successful multimillionaire and business entrepreneur who made a huge impact on my life. Thank you for caring enough to develop me at the very beginning of my Kirby career! Later, I continued growing under Mr. Windfeldt, the most successful Kirby executive and CEO of the Kirby Company within the one-hundred-year history. Added to this, special thanks go out to Jimmy Iorio. He is one of Kirby's greats and a Hall of Fame elite divisional supervisor. His special care for people, his passion, and his ability to help others is the best.

Another appreciative thanks is dedicated to Bud Miley, Kirby's current national and international worldwide president of field sales. His wit, communication skills, simplicity, and success exemplify the one-hundred-year-old company's standard of excellence. A special thanks goes to my loving and affectionate dear wife, Christine, my four beautiful children, and my grandchildren, who, through their faith, long-suffering, joy, love, kindness, self-control, patience, goodness, and peace (Gal. 5:22, 23), have applied to their wits an everlasting smile of positive encouragement to keep seeing this project completed.

Added to this heartfelt appreciation, I also thank my dear mother, Christine Jones. She is my *supermother.* Next, my brothers, Tonie and Larry, are dearly valued. Added to this list are my sisters, Sherlene, Bernita, Bertha, and late sister Bettie Herring. In addition, my extended brothers and sisters, Bernard, Wayne, Sharon, Gary, and Janice and my cousins, nephews, aunts, and uncles, far too many to mention, have my endless gratitude. In addition, I thank Cynthia Jenkins for serving as my book project manager. Most important, I want to thank Uncle Charles Lindberg "Lindsey" Webb for really making a difference in my life. Thanks, Unk! My appreciation extends to these close family and friends because their contributions helped my life evolve from a single story into the life-changing experience you are about to discover.

Now, in order to really appreciate CRAZY, allow your thinking to be synonymous to a laser-like focus. You will become so committed to the task until nothing distracts your eyes from the target. In other words, apply the five *P*s—prior, preparation, prevents, and poor performance—and finally also the four *F*s: be frank, fair, firm, and have fun! This is what *CRAZY* is all about!

PART I

Why You've GOT
to Be CRAZY!

Strength does not come from physical capacity.
It comes from an indomitable will.

—Mahatma Gandhi

When you think about what is crazy to the norm, this is the type of business we do. The norm is a basic prototype people can readily accept. For example, a retail business or sales business may have a commodity or product more readily accepted by the masses. Today's generation invests in technology, Internet, and social media with the hope that their ideas, business, and commodity will be accepted and adopted throughout the globe. However, the Kirby global company maintains a tried, tested, and proven success model for more than one hundred years.

In our business, what is crazy is to think you can sell a vacuum cleaner that costs what our product costs. Next, you go recruit people who believe they can have a good lifestyle with it. These people do not really want to sell at all. Then after they discover they have to go from door-to-door, they for sure do not want to go from door-to-door. Then you take the product out to the marketplace and show it to people who really don't want to buy it. Therefore, it is almost as if gravity were working against you. However, your belief system is so strong, and because of many successful examples, the program proves successful repeatedly. Thus, you believe mentally that you have already arrived. Then you decide, "This is what I am going to do!"

People arrive to our business from all sorts of diverse backgrounds. They succeed in a business where it appears the odds are really against them. Normally, a person would not want to do it anyway unless their family members supported them in the business. So team members work against all barriers, negatives, and things people claim cannot be done. It is not so much you have proven it. The example has been there for over one hundred years. People have done it prior to you. So therefore, you just go ahead and do it. You operate on blind faith until you deliver proven results.

A Former Veteran Starts a New Life

In my case, I did not have too much to hold on to. After serving in the military for four years, I returned from the armed forces in December 1971. To my surprise, I could not find a job that could pay me the income to take care of my family. The only job available paid minimum wage ($2.69 per hour) washing windows. I could not get enough out of that to take care of my family needs and weekly obligations. In addition, I could not create savings for the future. One day I saw an advertisement that said, "You can earn $250.00 a week! Call Mr. Jennings at 286-2231!" All I had to do was show a product fifteen times a week, and my manager would make sure I made $250 a week. Finally, I thought, *"I can get ahead of the curve!"* While shaking my head from side to side, I thought, "Boy, if this is true, I can really get ahead of the curve!" Fresh from the military, I knew how to work hard and accept authority. I knew how to follow directions. Therefore, if it could be done, I will do it and see if the program delivers what the advertisement promised. I called back with bountiful excitement. However, to my dismay, I learned the advertised positions were already filled. Upon returning home, I told my wife, "These were a bunch of prejudiced rednecks!" My attitude was not good at all. My wife encouraged me by saying, "Go back and tell them, if they give you a chance to work for them, YOU WILL become one of their best workers!" Thus, after pleading for the position, they gave me an opportunity to see what I could do. I promised that I would not let them down.

> *Some days I wouldn't sell. Some weeks I would not sell.*
> *However, I NEVER had a bad month.*
>
> *—Artis Webb*

What proved most phenomenal about my success that followed is that the outcome exceeded the expectation of what they said was possible! This outcome surprised me because I did not think I could sell. I just did not have a grateful attitude to convince me that "I could sell!" It has been said, "The harder you hit us and the deeper you drive us, the more peaceful it becomes." When I made the decision that this is the only thing I am ever going to do, my power arrived from a higher source.

Kirby initially turned me down because I did not have a "selling" or positive attitude. However, my wife continued to plead, "Go back and ask them!" Therefore, upon returning, they said, "We'll let you do it part-time." Following Kirby's green light to start as a dealer, I performed so well part-time that I thought, "If I am doing so well part-time, let me come in full-time?" Unbelievably, in forty-two years, I have never had a bad month (whereas I did not sell anything). Some days I would not sell. Some weeks I would not sell. One week I put on twenty-three presentations and did not sell anything. The next week I sold twenty-one Kirbys. So the product proved to be better than what the managers predicted! I never had a bad month in over forty years that could have prevented any sales to care for my obligations. My worst month in forty-two years was sixteen sales. This was my first month in sales. This amount equates to $5,000 gross profit in one month. That was my first month as a part-time dealer and the beginning of this so-called *CRAZY business*! Man, I am thankful and glad Mr. Jennings and Mr. Stewart gave me an opportunity to prove to myself and to my family that I have hidden talents and NBA (natural-born abilities) to become a superstar! Kirby provided me an opportunity to learn how to leverage my natural abilities that contributed to ultimate success.

All along I had everything required to
become a great salesman.

—Artis Webb

I always thought sales required communication and a belief that you can do it! Did I believe I could do it? Not necessarily, but I knew I could follow instructions and outwork most. I never realized I had interpersonal skills until I arrived to sales. In fact, in 1972, John Jennings, my distributor trainee, told me, "Artis, you have a very nice smile, you're very personable, and meet people very well. You have a million-dollar smile! With that, you can become a great success in Kirby!" On the outside, I exhibited signs to support my belief in this career. From that point forward, I would purposely display that smile, work hard to reflect a positive attitude, apply interpersonal skills, and before realizing it, I evolved into what they considered a GREAT salesperson!

On the inside, I continued to nurture a somewhat militant and bad attitude. For example, John Jennings was a white male. I say this because I automatically assumed he was prejudiced. My family was raised in a community of prejudiced people. Thus, my mother performed fieldwork and cleaned houses. This environment contributed to my inferiority complex and an inability to look people into their eyes. John Jennings continued to tell me that I could become successful. However, inside I really did not believe it because I failed to trust his advice. I continued to question his motives by asking myself. "Why is he telling me this?" He continued telling me this. So I thought, "What if this is true?" I am glad he saw more than I saw in myself. Thus, I immediately accepted him as my mentor and vowed to do whatever he suggested so I could make my life more complete. The outcome led to a new mind-set, drive, and name.

I earned the name Mr. Fantastic!

—*Artis Webb*

My factory distributor, Dave Stewart, called me Mr. Fantastic! Mr. Stewart delivered an interview to the Raleigh *Observer*. When the reporter asked how Kirby remained so successful in a down economy, he shared, "I have this guy named Artis Webb. He sells nine out of ten Kirby products shown." Therefore, when he called me Mr. Fantastic, I created an acronym as a guide to deliver outstanding service for my customers.

- F—*fascinate* customers. Keep it fun and upbeat.
- A—*above-average* presentations. Present the quality, reliability, and performance.
- N—*need* for it right now. Show customers how they benefit from features and benefits.
- T—*thinking* about the product during the presentation. Maintain an open mind.
- A—*answer* and anticipate questions in mind before they ask them. Always answer their questions.
- S—give them *satisfactory* answers. Never mislead customers. Always tell the truth.
- T—make sure their thoughts are *transferrable*. Inquire if they like it, want it, need it, or would use it. Do not force them to buy. Make sure it is their decision. Show them various ways they may be able to afford the product. Give different options for purchasing the product.
- I—*itemize* the budget. Explore what the customer can afford.
- C—ask for *cash*, *credit card*, or *check* or *contract*!

Isn't That Fantastic!

Thus, I had a way of showing it. Fantastic was my hook. I would show them the features and benefits, and I would say, "Isn't it fantastic!" Soon, customers would also think it is fantastic too. Then I learned that the more you get the customer involved, the more they start to see this as a show and have fun participating as you present the product. The people always enjoyed purchasing the product and recommending Kirby(s) to their friends. I knew if they did not buy it, there was a circumstantial situation that prevented them from buying. Some amazing aspects of the Kirby product are quality, reliability, performance, and lifetime rebuilding warranty. Consider how people stand in line to buy products, many of which are not of the same quality. I truly believe I am giving customers a service that is the best or better than anything on the market. We may use our phones and computers with a short-term warranty. However, how many of these products arrive with a lifetime warranty? Well, Kirby offers a lifetime rebuilding warranty that delivers a rebuilding guarantee for life! You will use it on a regular basis, and it is something that will last for a lifetime. Therefore, I never wanted to sell Kirbys if the original purchaser was not happy. However, it is one of the few products on the market that people will buy with a lifetime rebuilding warranty, and the company stands behind this promise.

So if you are nice to people, they will see your authenticity, because customers feel a sincere need to buy from people who are passionate about their product. Why Kirby? Because *K* stands for the "king of all vacuum cleaners," (*I*) it is *i*rresistible, (*R*) it is *r*eliable, and (*B*) it is the *b*est *b*uy and will last for (*Y*) *y*ears. If you are planning to purchase a complete home cleaning system, this product will last for years. Generation after generation will be yearning to use it repeatedly. When you have been on one side of the mountain, you keep climbing to get to the other side. The following acronym helped me climb to a side of success to build a foundation and successful business to support my family.

Commited, Regimented, Aspire, Zealous for Years

Now that is CRAZY! When you think of *crazy*, you think of people that are insane. The normal thought process is different. Therefore, when I apply CRAZY to this business, we could call this "thinking outside of the box." These individuals may reside inside insane asylums. People say "I am going to commit them" because they don't have the same natural "saneness" that the average person appears to have. People generally complete higher education or to the University of Kirby. It is not on the curriculum to become a "Kirbiologist" or a major in "Dirtology." We see this as the University of Kirby. You will learn the interpersonal skills. In addition, we will teach the technical skills required to work the business. However, when you start studying the business, you then become CRAZY. Because you first need to become totally *c*ommitted, *r*egimented, *a*spiring, and *z*ealous for *y*ears. Then continue to dream with your eyes open as you visualize. Then see your future unfold in front of you. Now that is my version of *CRAZY*!

Crazy Defined

Committed to the work. You were placed on this earth for three reasons: (a) to make a commitment to something, (b) to contribute to that commitment, and (c) then you have to grow. Therefore, you appear CRAZY in the sense that you are committed. To outside onlookers, regardless of the obstacles, you are so focused that you will stay committed to the task. Nothing can prevent success, because you have developed the drive attitude.

Regimentation, or discipline to do the same thing all the time. The process is similar to the military in the sense that you get up at the same time in the morning. Next, there is a program for exercise. You complete lunch at the same time, participate in certain activities, and then return to bed at the same time. Similarly, in our business, you place yourself on a discipline program to do the same thing, believing it will work out, taking advantage of the opportunity at hand.

Aspire to new heights. Observe examples of people who succeeded. Thus, you maintain a laser-like FOCUS (facing obstacles, countering unbelievable situations). Therefore, you stay focused and follow that one course until you succeed at it. Therefore, you do not place any limitations on what you can do. Keep aspiring! However and wherever that leads you, always measure from the point where you started to the point where you are. Never give up!

Zeal zest. You have that zeal and have that zest, that enthusiasm, and you believe success is going to happen. Allow that motivation to permeate you so others can see the charisma and excitement; the quality becomes transferrable. *Enthusiasm* is a godlike divine word. It comes from the word *ethos*, which means "god within"; you imitate that godly quality of enthusiasm within self. The motivation becomes contagious. The zeal is contagious: peers catch it, and customers are motivated by it. The last four letters of enthusiasm is *isam*, meaning "I am sold myself."

Years is the time invested to stick to this plan. You decide this will be my career and focus. People often say they have a plan B. However, I do not have a plan B. If I had a marriage plan B, I would not have remained committed to the present beautiful woman for forty-six years. There will always be a situation that does not work out. The greater you focus on creating success HERE, the greater your accomplishments will be! So if my plan A failed to work out, get another plan A until it works out. For example, you do not have a plan A life *and* plan B life. You live the best plan that a plan A life has to offer, and you do so to the fullest! You get a plan B life on this earth. So yearn to stay positive for years and years to come. Because it is you, you, you that matters. This will make the greatest difference in your ultimate plan.

Webb-Based Science Reflective Effective Audit

Ask yourself, do I have the fortitude of CRAZY—the drive and fearless mind-set to persist despite established norms? What can I do differently today to bring a solid winning attitude to the field? Write down the goals you have set to achieve on today and how you will persevere to deliver.

1.

2.

3.

CHAPTER 1

Inspiring Sales Leaders of Tomorrow

Motivation is everything. You can do the work of two people,
but you can't BE two people. Instead, you have to inspire the next
guy down the line and get him to INSPIRE his people.

—*Lee Iacocca*

My Generals

Mr. Webb leads a host of MRD rhinos and rhinettes. The leading five-star generals are distributor trainees: A. J. Webb, Yolanda Washington, Matt Edwards, Mehgan Webb, Herb Smith, Ed Sealy, Monroe and Aileen Edmonds, Darryl Walker, Tracie Bennett, etc.

I was fortunate to be a part of the organization that made me
the man I am today.

—*Ed Caldwell*

A shoulder injury led to Ed's meeting with Artis. In 1984, a friend was in Kirby during the holidays. Edward hurt his shoulders from playing tennis. Artis invited him to a sales meeting at 11:00 a.m. About thirty-eight minutes later, he knew this was his new career. Via this sales meeting, Edward learned he could earn $100,000 a year and live independently. Mr. Webb explained the opportunity, and the vision inspired him. During Ed's first month, he became the top dealer in the division. For example, he earned $3,000 over the first weekend. During this journey, Ed noticed some people were really stagnating due to a lack of vision. However, Ed always believed that the greatest nation is born from your *IMAGINATION*. He told Mr. Webb he would be promoted in ninety days and made it happen! Ed enjoyed the contact with people, knocking on doors, competitively; either you do it well, or you fail. Success is contingent upon your attitude. Whatever you believe one has or has not, the thoughts are constantly feeding your mind every day. Otherwise, the lack of ambition and attitude will nourish your thoughts. Mr. Webb invited a couple of speakers to come in, such as Ernie Villanueva. He was always great at having motivational speakers in and constantly reading. In time, Ed led his own team. Many people just sit by the wayside. Therefore, he volunteered to do it. Mr. Webb and Ed worked out together and ran at the gym. So what happens when you have a twenty-two-year-old person on fire? He was trying to harness the stallion, always out of control. However, because he produced, Mr. Webb let him get away with a few things. There is always a conflict of power. When you are twenty-three or twenty-four and someone says you can jump from on top of a building, you do not question it; you jump because you have allowed your inspiration to lead you. If you are fearful, rejection starts and proves disheartening. The real keys are the spirituality part within yourself and being humble. Added to these is feeding your mind constantly with the attitude of gratitude. The way you treat people is a key to continued success.

Mr. Webb came into my life and was willing to mold me. He touched many lives. I was fortunate to be a part of the organization that made me the man I am today! Mr. Webb will always be in some type of facet with people. He will always be able to touch people. Even though we were in groups and transitioned to greater roles, his training meetings always articulated a grounded message that a sales force could take to the field and achieve success. Mr. Webb could have become no. 1 in the world, but he strives to balance needs of the business with priorities of family and spirituality. Even though, when you check the status quo of people influenced in the Kirby Company, Mr. Webb is the no. 1 influencer, inspirer, and motivating distributor among his constituents. That is the positive influence life has generated over the years.

There Is a *Webb-Based* Science to Building Leaders of Tomorrow

Why do team members need to show up for work? These individuals show up for the SAME THINGS—*s*timulation, *a*ctivation, *m*otivation, *e*ducation, *t*raining, *t*eaching, *h*elping, *i*nspiring, *i*ncreasing *n*ew *g*raduates or *g*rowth *s*ales. Yes, that is keeping it real! We are staying green and growing rather than getting ripe and rot! We are ignorance on fire rather than knowledge on ice! I learned a quote from Willie Jolley: "We are constantly Learning, Editing, Aspiring, Presenting, Exhibiting, and Resourcifying." That is developing as a *leader*. We are ready to face it! That is, face your problems and acknowledge them, but do not let them master you! This excerpt comes from Mr. Willie Jolley's book *A Setback Is a Setup for a Comeback*. This quote I've held close to my personal philosophy. Thus, I have embellished and refined for my personal clarity.

Start Your Day

Get your whole mind, whole heart, and whole spirit into the game! Start early in the day, week, month, and year. You will stay ahead of the wave and learning curve.

Trace IT

Implies you are a great duplicator versus a great originator. Copy the original model to success without blemishes. Here is where problems originate. Discern what you can learn from the experience. Once is a mistake; twice is stupid. Finally, three times is just downright foolish. This enables you to reward your thinking and *play a more effective strategy* forward. Then fast-forward to stay in sync with your goals.

Erase IT

That is, learning from the mistake, make a commitment to do better in the future and let it go! There are two types of mistakes: those that teach and those that destroy. In other words, we can see those mistakes as learning experiences, or we can see them as deathblows. Make failure your teacher and not your undertaker.

Replace IT

Once you FACED IT, TRACED IT, and ERASED IT, you then must replace it. There will be people who will change things in your life that beg to be replaced. Do them a favor and grant them their wish; leave them alone and replace them. When we replace the negative element with a positive element and move to a place of peace, purpose, and passion (PPP), thereafter, we made a decision to be positive and focus on the positive rather than the negative. Within this place, you will find your ultimate reason to show up for work every morning. Why? Because you have to pursue your passion with a purpose and absolute confidence. Chase it differently! Then arrest it! Sentence it to life in prison or the death sentence for committing the crime of success. Make it a point to replace the old attitude by renewing the new attitude thought and refining and expanding your philosophy. Most important, make your dreams a reality by dreaming with your eyes wide open. This will prevent any stumbles or falls.

Visualize IT

What is the difference between a job, an opportunity, and a hustle? A job requires one to put in the time by clocking in and out. So when a team member arrives with this mentality, they will gauge or measure work by the amount of time or hours they work. The company will pay them so much per hour. In addition, they place time into a metric, which equates to a paycheck. However, a hustler wants to meet you in the field, place, or gathering. Team leaders will meet this person in the field because they are good at what they do. However, they never have the stability or sustainable success. These subleaders will put in some time and effort to get some results. Because these persons are not fully committed or progressed full circle in the program, they will only achieve "some results." However, a visionary person will arrive to Kirby with a perspective of requirements and equate these as their job description. Next, these winners will transfer that belief to an opportunity. This league of leaders believes, "I have to get good at this. I have to become good so I can teach it to others." Therefore, a visionary will strive not to measure outcomes by time and hours, but to mastery of their craft, always striving to achieve results. In a typical job, people are inclined to reflect selfish tendencies. For example, they may neglect teaching colleagues or teammates because they are afraid someone will take their position and knowledge from them. However, a visionary will embrace the opportunity and invest the time. This leader will measure success by results. The results and opportunities are unlimited and predicated on merchandise sold, products, and abilities to produce, inspire, train, teach, and close for other people.

With a hustle, there is no reward or fulfillment. One is merely focused on the reward for the day or moment. One might continue for a day, month, years, and yet still end up with a hustle. With a job, your earnings are limited by a forty-hour focus and paycheck. However, an opportunity maintains no boundaries. A sales leader must remember that a person with a vision of the opportunity exudes self-sufficiency, self-motivation, unlimited vision, and a mind-set that is legacy focused. They view risk as a complement to their success. Pursuing an opportunity requires an intestinal fortitude, the ability to lead and produce results. No one can accurately measure a person's vision. Only an individual can accomplish this alone. However, the visionary sales leader will allow other team members to learn the secrets of their success. The team's success is predicated on your ability to make them better. Remember, in business, you get either better from your journey or bitter from your lack of learning.

Embrace IT

Do you believe in the power of one? Not just the number but also the POWER that the no 1 represents? Do you believe one idea, one moment, one decision, and one person can *be* that powerful? *I BELIEVE you can be that person.* You have the God-given potential to use your influence to affect others, shape the future, change lives, and make an external difference as you become internally fortified. I have experienced how seemingly ordinary people applied their influence to accomplish extraordinary things, which result in a powerful impact on others. However, the results depend upon HOW you apply your potential. You have the same potential. If you doubt that one person can make a difference, take note.

- *Winston Churchill* convinced England they could survive the Nazi war machine, and they did.
- *Vince Lombardi* turned the Green Bay Packers from NFL doormats into legends. They won championships!
- *Lee Iacocca* turned Chrysler around and saved the company from bankruptcy.
- *Barack Obama* became the first African American president. He won two terms.
- *Jesus Christ, firstborn of all creation*—the power of one!

These are just a few examples of how the power of one made a difference. Go BE a champion, make a difference, and because of the power of one great idea, you can transform your team of leaders into champions of the future.

POM (Peace of Mind)

This arrives as an outcome or the essence of your success. The Kirby business requires a determined mind-set, vision, and desire to do better. Keep inching yourself out of it, and before you realize it, you will move from a forty-dollar-a-month apartment into a beautiful home. The journey can be compared to learning how to walk. Over time, you will move by taking one step at a time. This does not seem like a big deal, because you have worked so hard and worked through the graduation and transformation. One day you do not have confidence, and the other day you do. Come what may, Mr. Webb never sees himself the way others perceive him. He is always working on something, so he never feels like he is a finished product. Fear of failing drives Mr. Webb to work hard with an unstoppable spirit. Even if he should fail, he wants to look back with a peace of mind knowing he did his very best. Because he believes, the

softest pillow to lay your head on at night is one with a good conscience, knowing
he left everything in the ring. That is the JOY of the Kirby business—*journeying
over yonder!* This means making a complete transformation and feeling good
about the journey (business accomplishments and time invested with family).
A new birth to success requires one to remain alert to constantly renewing
success! In addition, remain passionate about creating success for your team.

Know Your STAR Power

One of the greatest gifts and talents we as distributors or leaders possess is
the ability to define our "STAR power"! This power is *s*tickability, *t*arget point,
*a*ction plan, *r*esolution, and *r*esults. Your star power represents and becomes
your future or "futuristic power" in order to succeed. Remember, defining your
star power helps you define what is possible today, because you must act within
this space mentally before you arrive physically.

- Knowing the future is difficult. You have to create a defined and
  redefined plan.
- Controlling the future is impossible. So prepare for your triumphs.
- Knowing today is essential. Therefore, work each day as if it was your
  last opportunity to make a difference to leave a legacy.
- Finally, enduring the challenge is growth. Celebrate the differences
  and appreciate your star power.

This Is WHY!

If your *why* doesn't make you cry, then your *why* is not emotionally connected
to your passion. Controlling today is impossible, because success is a result of
continued action filled with continual adjustments. The greatest challenge
you will ever face is that of expanding your mind and consciousness. It is
like crossing the great frontier, you must be willing to be a pioneer, to enter
unchartered territory, to face the unknown, and to conquer your own fears,
uncertainties, doubts, and skepticisms (FUDS). However, here is the good news.
When you change your thinking, you change your life, and it will "get better
when you get better." As Oliver Wendell Holmes remarked, "A man or woman's
mind, once stretched by a new idea, never regains its original dimension." When
you want to expand your capacity, the first place to start is always in your mind.
That is the only place you can practice "perfectly" without making mistakes.
Remember, the purpose of this philosophy is to define your star power, then
develop team members into distributor trainees and distributors as soon as you

and their maturation process allow you to do so. Then you know how to increase your capacity for action.

When you want to expand your potential and your capacity, you must change your thinking. For example, expand your mind from recruiting dealers to recruiting distributor trainees and distributors. This is a philosophical paradigm shift. However, when you change *only* your thinking and neglect to change your actions, you will fall short of your potential. To start expanding your capacity (to develop more dealers and team leaders), take the following three steps:

- STOP doing only things that you know does not work. START evolving with more creativity and innovative approaches and remaining open to experiences, challenges, and ideas.
- STOP doing what is expected and START doing more than expected (i.e., requires some elaboration, etc.).
- STOP doing important things occasionally and START doing important things daily. Again, be creative to new endeavors.

The result is your own personal reciprocation and development. One of the greatest rewards of promoting distributor trainees or refinement of our future power is occasionally hearing someone positively impacted by a coworker's influence. Recently I received calls from Leon Thomas, Andre Lunn, Ed Caldwell, Andra Williams, Daniel Brown, and Derek McCune, just to name a few. They called and shared their appreciation for working with them and sharing the programs that help them become a distributor or have a very successful endeavor. General George Patton once said, "The greatest of all miracles is that we need not be tomorrow what we are today. However, we can improve when we make use of the potential implanted in us by God." Make sure you give yourself an effectiveness audit so you can be sure what you are thinking works. Instead, do more work, because if you are not doing something with your life, it does not matter how long it will last! Ask yourself the question Benjamin Franklin asked every day in the morning: "What good shall I do in this day?" When the evening arrived, he inquired, "What have I done today?" Then map out a new plan to achieve greater success on tomorrow!

GO Create IT! In Success, Become or Be!

S	STEADFAST!
U	UNDERSTAND YOUR OBSTACLE!
C	CLEAR YOU MIND OF SELF-DOUBT!

C	CREATE A POSITIVE MENTAL PICTURE!
E	EMBRACE THE CHALLENGE!
S	STAY ON TRACK!
S	SHOW THE WORLD!

In $UCCE$$ . . .

The most important letters in the word *success* are *U* and *E*. Why? Because you (*U*) have to earn (*E*) the right to have it! This is sometimes measured by money. Be and stay conditioned for success.

- Exercise thirty minutes a day.
- Envision and record personal goals for the day.
- Consider what amount of coaching, training, and leadership you need to reach these goals.
- Select motivational books from Webb's recommended reading to galvanize your mind-set to success.

Go Inspire IT!

What makes you feel good is a positive attitude. Alternatively, what makes you great is the pain, doubt, failure, suffering, and adversity. Challenges of overcoming personal obstacles can fail to inspire. Character is not made out of sunshine and roses. Like steel, this quality is refined by fire, between the hammer and the anvil. Remember, you are responsible for your attitude, aspirations, and for promotional opportunities. IF you recognize how responsible you are to yourself, this business will be simple and achievable.

So if you ever get despondent, remember your affirmation agreement. This sales mission statement will *tell you that you deserve more!* Every decision you have made so far came from the thoughts in your mind. This requires a little discipline in developing your brainpower. If you read your affirmation agreement for six weeks, every single morning and evening, you will become a 100 percent different person. You will love yourself more as a person. Next, you will believe in yourself, become more confident, and create incredible and increased success!

Control Time Effectiveness

Remember, life is consumed by seconds and minutes. You have only 60 seconds in a minute, 60 minutes in an hour, 1,440 minutes in a day, and 86,400 seconds in a day. For example, if you decide to invest four minutes a day staring into space, within one year's time, this habit will equate to a total of twenty-four hours of wasted time. Yes, just a tiny little minute, but an eternity is in it. Therefore, remember time slips away in seconds, drifting away in minutes, and drawn away into days. Then suddenly we arrive to the place called years, until LIFE has dealt us a hand we wish we could trade in. Remember, a goal not set is a goal not met. A goal not met is a goal not set. Therefore, TAKE CONTROL! Now is the time for YOU to come to the aid of your own success. To succeed, to thrive, and to live the life of your dreams, you have to be willing to risk failure and rejections and keep going. Keep moving and fighting, then you too will experience the sweet smell of success, because you were first willing to experience the joy of failure. Without risk, there is no reward!

Webb-Based Science Reflective Effective Audit

Team leaders and managers, how will you inspire your team to greater success today? What will YOU do differently to help build their careers? Write down the goals you have set to achieve on today.

1.

2.

3.

CHAPTER 2

History of a Sales Legend

*I transformed frustration and pain into
inspirational motivation.*

—*Artis Webb*

Before exploring the success and business part of Artis's story, here is a little about where his dedication, discipline, drives, and desire was born. Artis was born on June 16, 1948, in a small rural community of Pea Ridge near the Albemarle Sound. This little town is located in Washington County, North Carolina. The population of this community in which Artis grew up was very scarce. There were so few people that the area does not have traffic lights. He attended an elementary school in Creswell, North Carolina. According to the United States Census, the population of the city was less than two thousand in 2010 (US Census 2010). The village of Pea Ridge contained less than 325 households. Because of strong racial prejudice, opportunities did not come about until the mid '60s. When young adults finished high school or dropped out of school, they left the area. Added to this, a lack of a strong economy and agricultural area resulted in the only remaining work of farm (picking cotton, priming tobacco, and picking tomatoes, etc.) fieldwork. We definitely could not find opportunities as receptionists or cashiers.

According to the 2010 United States Census, the poverty rate for Washington County was 25.2 percent, compared to North Carolina at 16.1 percent and the United States poverty rate being 14.3 percent. The county maintained a wealth of black uneducated people largely related to few jobs and an above-average poverty rate in Washington County.

As the eldest son, Artis struggled along with his mother, a single mom. Growing up in a household without a father, he grew up extremely poor. Ms. Christine Webb's fight against poverty was real, not imaginary hardships. Such challenges included economic and social battles. The environment at home proved even more dysfunctional. At a young age, Artis regularly witnessed alcohol, abuse, and battered women abused within his own home. These acts were very painful for Artis. Nevertheless, he vowed to make a better life for his family. Moreover, his tenacious mother performed menial housework and agriculture fieldwork to earn a living for her family. This environment began the building work for this future entrepreneur and driven sales executive talent, Artis Webb!

My First Mentors: Elder James A. Moore and Mr. Robert L. Webb

Preacher James Moore (cousin) and his son-in-law, Robert Webb, forged a strong driving force in the life of Artis Webb. The Reverend James Moore was an entrepreneur who provided farm labor work for black folks in the community of Pea Ridge and surrounding area. Working for large farmers, James Moore delivered manual labor to harvest crops, such as potatoes, cabbage, cucumbers, and snap peas. Preacher Moore (as he was called) was dedicated to helping people in the community. Living on a rural farming section of the northeastern coast, farmwork was plentiful and wages were cheap. Thus, he organized farm labor by buying a bus and providing dependable transportation to and from work. This type of seasonal work enabled men, women, and children to supplement their incomes. In addition, these families were able to survive on the provision they obtained from governmental welfare programs. Children were especially happy to work in the agriculture field as this resource provided money to buy school clothes and supplies. One such child was Artis Lee Webb. Seasonal work created such a huge demand that Rev. Moore invited his son-in-law, Robert Webb, to help him provide this service. Robert married Rev. Moore's daughter Marie. His professional career was a truck driver in the log woods industry. During farming season, Robert quit driving trucks to devote energies to growing seasons that lasted a few months, from May to October. In addition, he would contract work from various farmers. Thus, Robert Webb became a self-made entrepreneur and businessperson. As such, he quickly realized the value of providing bulk labor that could finish a job in a timely manner. As a result, he was able to negotiate higher wages for farmworkers.

Connecting the Dots of Discipline

James Moore and Robert Webb not only worked in eastern parts of North Carolina, but they also migrated to Maryland and other states on the Eastern Seaboard to work in the tomato factories. Artis and his mom, Christine Webb, were often included in this group of migrant workers. At an early age, Artis's mother instructed and disciplined him to work hard for long hours and execute quickly. For example, Artis ran to return baskets used to contain the product harvested—potatoes, cucumbers, or tomatoes. As a single parent, his mother's obligations required dual deliveries normally expected of two parents. With strong determination, his mother persevered with pride and a competitive spirit. Working alongside his mother, Artis inherited these traits, followed her example, and applied these competencies to create a successful career as a determined sales executive.

Building a Means to Support Family

As the oldest son, Artis's mother explained why they could not afford to run out of containers that held the products. This outcome would be a serious waste and misuse of time, and so time was very valuable. Most children do not know and recognize when they are poor. To the contrary, Artis did. The Negro educator Booker T. Washington encouraged blacks to pull themselves up by their bootstraps. Well, Artis did not always have boots. He had to grab his ankles to pull himself up. His competitive spirit and desire to win provided him with the motivation to succeed. Artis was always ready to accept a challenge. The state welfare system did not give much more than food. As Artis was the oldest, there was not much handed down to him. My grandfather, Rev. Moore, encouraged young kids to work hard. Added to this, even as an old man, he challenged us to pick up more tomatoes than he could. Thus, the race was on! About twenty young boys ranging from twelve to fifteen years of age worked hard to see who picked the most tomatoes. Who do you think won this race? Your guess is correct. The winner was Artis Webb! He was always the only young man that picked more tomatoes than Rev. Moore did. Harvesting one hundred baskets of tomatoes, Artis proudly delivered ten dollars to his mother for one day's work. The seeds of desire to win were planted into Artis Webb at a very young age.

Julius Webb, First Cousin and Mentor

Like Jack, Julius Webb was Artis's first cousin. He is four years older than Artis. When Julius reflects upon the upbringing of both him and Artis, his stories reveal a family committed to taking care of immediate and extended family. There were different children family siblings who grew up together in one house. Julius's mother and Artis's mother were sisters (both had ten kids). Julius is Artis's first cousin. Artis's grandmother had twenty-five children organized into three different families in one home. As those siblings became older, they left and moved to New York, Virginia, and many other parts of the country. There were different family siblings who grew up together in one house. Julius, his mother, and his siblings, were the ones left in the house while Artis, his mother, and his sibling were growing up.

Aunt Florence (Julius's mother) was mulatto. Thus, Julius's mother was light-skinned. Julius's father was not there either. Therefore, you had two single moms raising their kids. Julius took the lead in his family. Artis took the lead in his family. Jack lived down the road with his parents. Artis, his mother, brothers, and sisters lived together in one room. Thus, it was no surprise to see the similar arms of support within the Webb family. Artis and Julius emerged from small and humble beginnings, a household with three different families. As mentioned, Artis, along with several other siblings, stayed in a back room. Another aunt came over and lived upstairs. The house was old, unstructured, and physically unstable. Julius can still remember when someone fell through the cracks. Six years ago, the city condemned and wanted to tear the house down. The house had a history of families coming and going. We called it a "bootleg" house because they sold whiskey to survive. On the weekends, Artis and Julius endured parties. People arrived Friday through Sunday to party with tunes from our jukebox. Julius served as the bartender. Artis and Julius shared with their grandfather's custom to have one shot of whiskey in the morning to keep colds (or sicknesses away).

Out of the various siblings, no one had ever gone to college. Julius was the first to achieve this accomplishment. However, Julius notes if it were not for a committed and intentional president (Dr. Ridley) of Elizabeth City State College, he may never have decided to go to college, majored in sociology, and later served as a school counselor, assistant principal, director, and today education advocate. Julius and Artis watched the effect alcohol had on the people who would party at their home every weekend. People would get drunk and wake up in the home. Amazing none of these strangers harmed their sisters. Artis and Julius shared a very good relationship as cousins. In fact, he cannot remember if they have ever had a disagreement. Artis graduated, left home, and moved to New York with his uncle Charles Lindberg "Lindsey" Webb. Later he left for the United States Air Force and served for four years. Julius graduated and worked in New York. For almost two years, Julius reported to Artis, after he came out of the military or armed forces, as a new dealer with Kirby. Although he enjoyed making money selling with Artis, he eventually returned to his true passion of teaching middle-school math, culture, and science.

Christine Jones, Artis's Mother

According to Artis's mother, an eighty-six-year-old black female that is very healthy both mentally and physically, her son Artis always practiced affecting people positively. In grade school, Artis was very smart. He made nothing but As on his report card. Artis's scholastic ability attracted the attention of some of his teachers. Artis's mother, being a seasonal worker, was often required to migrate to different states such as Florida and the eastern shores of Maryland and Delaware. When school was in session, Artis's mother would leave him to stay with a teacher until the season was over. Paulette N. Hill remembered that Artis was very humble, likable, and shy, and he stayed to himself. He would help by pumping and bringing in the water along with firewood. Artis's workload included helping Reverend Otis "Uncle Buddy" Norman with farmwork. Artis and Paulette's strong friendship developed because of their childhood experiences.

One quality Artis's mother will never forget is the promise he gave at sixteen years of age: "Artis promised me that he would buy me a home when he was old enough to get a job." She always knew that Lee had the traits and the intellectual ability for greatness, after all, his grandmother on his father's side, Mrs. Annie Blount, was a schoolteacher. Little did she know that her son would not only make good on his promise to buy her a house, but would also have a positive effect on his siblings by providing them with a summer job and buying their school clothes. This continued until they became adults. Ms. Christine Jones, Artis's mom, cherished the relationship between herself and Lee's wife, Christine. When visiting her son, Artis would often tell his wife, Christine, "Go take Momma shopping."

Artis's mom has a wealth of creative talent as a great cook, a good tailor, and a hair stylist. Thus, it was no surprise to see Artis apply his inherited creative powers to become a success with the Kirby Company. Julius remembers Artis's creative and competitive talents revealed in his belief that he could outdance Julius. Those were some of the funniest moments growing up together. Despite limited resources, Julius and Artis prospered during controversial times. They did not experience racial turmoil where they lived. In 1975, the North Carolina schools system began to integrate. Julius became more aware that racism had a face when he started marching to integrate the downtown theater to educate children about white and black persons who contributed to society. Julius extends his appreciation to Artis for allowing him to work at Kirby for a short time frame while he built a path back to his true passion of teaching.

We groomed Artis in dedication, discipline, drive, and desire.

—Jack Webb

There are so many rags-to-riches stories in America. The welfare-to-wealth story of Artis Webb has to rank in the top 5 percent. As mentioned, a wealth of events during childhood proved painful for Artis. Thus, he vowed to make a better life for his family. Artis kept his promise. He provided financial and emotional stability for his mother and siblings while taking care of his own family. Artis purchased an above-average upscale home for his mother and younger siblings (valued at $100,000). Over the years, he has been a source of employment and role model for his immediate and extended family.

After serving four years in the military, Artis Webb took it upon himself to go out and find a job to provide for his family. He started cleaning windows for $2.69 per hour. Artis Webb is a dedicated husband, father, entrepreneur, promoter, consultant, distributor, investor, motivational speaker, and business owner. Most men have a common goal. Some want to be rich and famous, and others want to be business owners, good fathers, husbands, and even ministers of God. Nevertheless, have you ever met a man that owned all these tasks by making time for each one to the best of his ability and not failing in any areas? Very few people would want the responsibility of all this, but there is one man that takes it on full force, with wisdom, vision, and courage. His name is Artis Webb! Artis worked at the Durham Research Triangle Area, barely making enough to get by, washing windows. Next, Artis discovered what would become his passion and dream career. One simple advertisement in the paper would determine his financial success from this point forward.

Wearing his big 'Fro and huge amount of pride, Artis walked into a Kirby office for an interview. He was turned down cold and not accepted. This though was not going to be acceptable to him. He continued to go back to the Kirby office where they told him that he would have to be a part-time dealer. Artis accepted this, and his first month in the business, though part-time, sold sixteen Kirbys. Not stopping there, from his second month all the way to his seventh month, he sold over twenty-four Kirbys a month with a high month of thirty-three sales, earning his Five-Diamond Medallion and his President's pen.

Within the first eleven months, Artis was promoted to a (DT) distributor trainee in Burlington/Graham, North Carolina. The role is comparable to a purchasing agent for a CEO. If you compare this role to one in corporate, a distributor tells the CEO what they do through purchasing merchandise. They teach them the full spectrum of the business. Distributors buy products from the CEO, he gets it at factory price, and distributors gain the products at wholesale price. Thus, his efforts in his newfound niche continued to pay off as he only moved up in the business. However, Webb's hopes and dreams came to a screeching halt when a group burned his office down in 1974. This tragic and racist act put a lot of fear, uncertainty, doubt, skepticism, anxiety, and frustration into Webb's heart. He lost his entire organization, inventory, customers' machines for service, and his financing, and he had threats from the IRS to padlock his office because of not paying his taxes. Yet Webb found a way to turn his frustration and pain into inspiration and motivation. With heart, desire, determination, and a whole lot of confidence combined, Webb received help from his distributor Mr. Stewart. Thus, he went out by himself and presented 105 presentations and sold 105 Kirbys in a row. What made this outcome so astounding is that he sold these 105 Kirbys via cash, check, or credit cards, because he had no one to finance his contracts. This proved to be Webb's most outstanding achievement as a dealer, distributor trainee, and confidence builder. Just as one very popular song by the group McFadden and Whitehead (1981) acclaimed, this gave Artis the vision that "Ain't no stopping me now, I'm on the move!"

Promotion after promotion, Webb continued to improve his craft, growing as a businessperson and in self-development. First, he accomplished 45 sales his first month as a field supervisor and 105 sales his top month. As a distributor (DT), Artis had a high month of 127 sales. In 1977, he gained a promotion to factory distributor, soaring to over 414 sales as the no 1 distributor in the division for over five consecutive years. He achieved his long-term goal of being able to provide his mother with a beautiful home (valued at $100,000+) equipped with eleven rooms and three and a half bathrooms on a one and half acres of land. Interestingly so, this home was the same house that his mother earned a living in cleaning and serving another family.

In 1988, Artis accepted another promotion as an outreach distributor to Kirby World Headquarters. Next, in 1992, he accepted another promotion as national sales manager for the entire world of Kirby. Thus, he moved his family to Cleveland, Ohio. Dedication to this promotion included eight years, traveling to over fifty states and seventy-plus countries, inspiring and motivating the world of Kirby. Thus, Artis successfully provided a positive and inspiring legacy for young and old to follow.

After achieving such accomplishments, Artis decided to move back to the south and step down from such a time-consuming career, and he became a divisional supervisor. A divisional supervisor governs four of five states (four hundred to six hundred people). Artis sold thousands as a divisional supervisor. He motivated his team to excel in this way. Within three years, he accomplished eight BMIBs (best months in business) as a divisional supervisor. After watching the success achieved in Kirby, his children desired to enter the business. His youngest daughter, Mehgan, could easily depart and become a chief of sales strategy for corporate. In addition, his son A. J. also delivers executive level talent comparable to a chief and people development officer. Lastly, his oldest daughter, Yolanda, would make an excellent chief marketing officer (CMO). Added to these strengths, his other son Aaron Webb would make a great chief customer and consumer advocate.

AJ and Mehgan expressed strong desires to exhibit Kirby excellence as demonstrated by their father, Artis Webb. Thus, they are on a path to become distributors. In addition, Yolanda continues to support the operations side of the business while building her own enterprise in entertainment branding. Thereafter, Artis resigned as a supervisor and decided to go back to being a full-time family man and factory distributor for Kirby.

Webb has accomplished so much, paving the way for aspiring Kirby dealers, showing them that there is a dream that is attainable to all who truly desire it. Winning over fifteen national contests as a distributor and being one of the top fifty distributors for four years, attaining the Golden Circle status (the million-dollar club) while planning to promote twelve more distributors on top of his existing nine. There are so many accomplishments that time would escape us to mention them all. However, these accomplishments remain unforgettable and well appreciated. Artis has taken the responsibility upon himself to take care of his immediate family and his extended family of Kirby by training, teaching them how to retrieve what it is that they truly want and desire. It takes a huge amount of character to say that you are the kind of person that would give up all your time and effort for the success of others, even when they are not blood related.

Now you can see why Artis Webb is known around the GLOBE as the Head Rhino! He refers to himself as Dr. Done, "CURE ALL OBJECTIONS, AND LEAVE NONE!" Because Kirby is the Great Equalizer! As Artis is dedicated to all aspects of his life, doing each fully and wholeheartedly, I am honored to introduce to you the great legend, Artis Webb, the HEAD RHINO!

Webb-Based Science Reflective Effective Audit

Team leaders and managers, ask yourselves, How I will inspire my team to greater success today? What will I do differently to help build their careers? Write down the goals you have set to achieve on today.

1.

2.

3.

CHAPTER 3

Running a Business Is about Commitment to Family

The journey is the thing.

—Homer

The culture of a typical American family is to grow up, decide if you will complete your education or not, then start your own business or work to build *another person's company*. However, when you walk inside Webb's office, you will see something unique, special, and the visual will leave an unforgettable impression and teach an important lesson about family. First, you will see an African American family working and *staying together* in the same business. Within the front office, be sure to notice a focused mother running the bookkeeping and financial matters. At 9:00 a.m. sharp, do not miss the enthusiasm of a daughter leading daily sales meetings. Added to these is a brother who inspires teams and customers with his excelling quality of leadership and client management. In addition, besides the mother, catch a glimpse of another daughter who leads the company in marketing strategy. This is the Webb family business and enterprise. You will become amazed at the leaders behind the phenomenal Artis Webb and their personal words of appreciation for the Head Rhino.

From Christine Webb, with Love

Artis would have made it without my support. I am glad I didn't give him a chance to find out whether he could or not.

—Christine Webb

Do you know where you want to go? Do you know where your road is leading? Well, in February 1972, Artis was discharged from the air force. Artis answered an advertisement in the newspaper, which read, "You can earn $250.00 a week." In answering that advertisement, we chose a road that would lead us to financial security with opportunities to travel and meet wonderful people like ourselves all over the world of Kirby. However, it was not easy, and it was not always happy times. Thus far, you have heard Artis's story. Now I am honored to share mine.

I was happy when Artis told me he found a job where he could make good money—because we really needed it. We just had our first child, and money was tight. After training, Artis set out that weekend, and together we sold three Kirbys. Even though I did not personally demonstrate the Kirbys, I was physically there; my heart and soul were present. When Artis returned home at night, I always thought it was important to wait up for him. To facilitate these moments, I rearranged my daughter's schedule. She was only two months old, another challenge during that time. However, I thought it was important that she be awake when her daddy arrived home. It was important to me that they have to know each other. Therefore, when he got home, he got to play with her and put her to bed while I warmed his food. Although my words did not express support, warming his food and listening to the going on(s) of the day were my way of saying, "I love you and will support you." So many young men and women on the road to success in Kirby do not make it because they did not have the support needed at home. The word *support* means to "hold up, to aid or assist in standing, or just to be there," and that was my goal. I believed that Artis would have made it with or without my support because that is the kind of person he is, but I am glad I didn't give him a chance to find out whether he could or not.

I learned every component required to run a
successful business.

—Christine Webb

Therefore, right from the beginning, Artis sold many Kirbys, and we made a lot of money. After we received our distributorship, I quit my job as a claims adjuster for Blue Cross and Blue Shield to work for Artis in his office. As we had never worked together before, it was a real test. There were times when we wanted to kill each other, but we worked it out. I came to appreciate my husband's strong qualities as a leader and motivator. Therefore, instead of trying to be his equal in the business, which causes most of the problems, I decided to be one of his students and learn from him, and I did. I also educated myself on areas of the business that I thought could enable me to help the most. Therefore, I learned bookkeeping and how to interact with people such as our banker, CPA, lawyer, and accountant. I learned to deal with these four people, and they became friends. This relieved Artis to focus on what he does best—sales and motivating people. I learned to sell Kirbys too! Thus, I earned my Five-Diamond Medallion and three legs on my President's Pen. In Kirby, the Five-Diamond Medallion is awarded to a dealer who sold fifteen Kirbys a month for five months. Added to this award is the President's Pen, an award and honor provided when a dealer sells twenty-four Kirbys in one month and on their own. I received this award because I accomplished this success three months in a row. In addition, I also learned to recruit one-on-one and complete small repairs on Kirbys. My goal was to let Artis know that I loved him and wanted to support him so that we could truly say, "*We* did it together!" I sold enough Kirbys with my team to win a trip to Bermuda. Artis and I had a fantastic time! We worked hard and played hard!

We weathered a lot of hard and sad times together.

—Christine Webb

Even the second-wisest man to walk the earth (King Solomon) said, "Two are better than one . . . because they have a good reward for their hard work, for if one of them should fall the other one can raise his partner up. In addition, if two lie down together, they also will certainly get warm. And if somebody could overpower one alone, two together could make a stand against him." Therefore, this is what Artis and I delivered. Together we accomplished a lot. We weathered many hard and sad times together. For example, once his mother's house burned clear to the ground. Therefore, we made a decision to help. While Artis invested time to support and help buy his mother a new house, I stayed and ran the office. I was always on the lookout for a man who cared about his mother. Because this showed me he would care about the mother of his children. Artis is that high caliber and quality of man. The saddest hour in Kirby arrived one day after I dropped my daughter off to school. I returned home and realized immediately that Artis was not home. I did not smell his Obsession cologne that he put on every morning after taking a shower. It is amazing how we travel through life, experience great things, but pay little attention to the details. When these things are missing, we know how important they are to our happiness. Well, not smelling his Obsession cologne (that indicates his presence), I knew immediately that something was wrong. So I asked my nephew (who lived with us), "Where is Artis?" He followed me upstairs, out of the earshot of my two boys, who at the time were eleven and seven, and my daughter Mehgan, who was ten months old, to inform me that the hospital called to say a car hit Artis while he was jogging!

I will not let you choke . . . and die on me

—*Christine Webb*

Well, it was at that moment I thought my life would end. However, I knew I had to hold things together and think positive! I called the hospital, afraid to ask how he was doing, to make sure he was still alive. I asked the nurse if she would go and ask him a question for me, and she said YES! Thank God, I knew he was spared alive, and when she came back with an answer, I knew he was conscious. When I first saw Artis in the emergency room, I almost did not recognize him because he looked so broken in spirit. Still, if we had experienced an accident with a car, we would probably look the same. I was taken back because I had never seen my strong and confident husband look like this before. We got through it! While Artis was recuperating from his accident, suffering a broken jaw that had to be wired shut for three months, I ran back and forth from the house to the office, from holding sales meetings in the morning to feeding him milk shakes with a syringe. The day I brought him home from the hospital, the doctor told me to make sure he did not choke on his vomit. He said if he should vomit, I had to cut the wires with some little scissors that would not cut paper. So on the way home, I told Artis not to vomit, "Because I will snatch this wire out of your mouth and take your teeth with it! I will not let you choke on your vomit and die on me"; he decided to drive to help take his mind off the possible dilemma.

While stepping up to the plate, I followed Artis's
direction to the letter.

—*Christine Webb*

During those days, I learned a lot while facilitating sales meetings for Artis. We went through archives of information, and he wrote things down for me to do. I followed his direction to the letter. When you follow directions from leadership, then no doubt you will become successful. Successful people follow directions and do what other successful people do. Well, Artis recovered, and even though our sales dropped drastically while he was recuperating, we eventually got them back up through hard work and doing the things we knew we needed to do. On the way back up, we received a visit from Jimmy Iorio, an outreach distributor during this time with Kirby. He really showed us that he cared about us. We developed a stronger friendship that will last forever. That is what Kirby has done for us. This company helped us meet people and create friendships with people whom we would not have met otherwise. Later Artis received a position as national sales manager at Kirby World Headquarters.

As a family, we talked about this and decided to take this road, which led to so many places that Artis earned enough sky miles to go to the moon. During his national sales manager tenure, Artis and I tried to touch people's lives and make them better, not just in Kirby, but across their total lives. We believe that people can do anything IF they believe they can. During this time, people often asked, "How do you put up with all of Artis's travels and being away from you?" My response was, "*We chose this journey.* In February 1972, I promised him that I would support him, and that is how I can do it. I still take him to the airport every time he has to go. It does not matter how late or how early, and I pick him up every time he returns, no matter how late or how early, because we are in this TOGETHER!" This year, we will celebrate our forty-sixth anniversary and look forward to where we will go.

In closing, I believe the basic for all achievement is a passionate desire, and I have never seen anyone pursue success with the passion, emotion, intenseness, and caring more than Artis. I believe if you are a dealer, team leader, distributor, trainer, field supervisor, divisional supervisor, national sales manager, wife, or significant other, to really succeed and succeed in a BIG way, then you are all under obligation to support the efforts and expectations of your great leaders within this great company. Remember, to succeed, you have to plan for it and plan for it together, because two are always better than one.

Many of us received conditioning to wait for something to be handed to us, or take whatever is given to us. However, the Webbs have instilled a culture of strong connection to family, having each other's backs, and having a strong drive to build their own enterprise. The will to deliver this outcome starts from within. Sometimes we reflect back and wonder, Why did Artis receive the position of national sales manager, an opportunity to inspire others to greater heights? As you can see, we invested in building a new mind-set and environment within our home. What happens when the next generation receives exposure to positive motivation, support, and doors of opportunity at a young age? Well, our children will share their stories and appreciation for their upbringing.

A Second Generation Inspired by the Head Rhino

Yolanda Belser, Marketing Manager and CEO of YSquare Management

> *Being raised in a positive environment is unique for an
> African American family. Because of our struggles,
> sometimes we don't get that.*
>
> —*Yolanda Belser*

As the oldest child, Yolanda came along during a time when Webb was just getting started in the Kirby business. With a huge amount of reflection, candor, and admiration for her parents, Yolanda provides her perception and value for the evolution of this Kirby family.

From Yolanda, with gratitude!

I did not realize the depth of financial distress for my family. For example, I was told my bed resided inside a drawer. I did not have a crib. We lived in a one-bedroom room without a lot of heat, with poor conditions. The monthly rent was forty dollars. Therefore, the first thing I remember from my family is a lot of love. As a little girl, my father told me, "Anything Yolanda wants, she can get." Some of the things I gained from that are strong determination and thick skin. They call my dad the Head Rhino because of the thick skin. Tenacity helps me today, because I own my own talent brand management and entertainment company. It is a very humble business. Money arrives after you have invested time . . . then presented it to the world. It was hard and fun. I found that aspect appealing. At the age of seven, I started doing hair. After graduating from high school with a cosmetology license, I obtained my license and started working at eighteen. At the age of twenty-four, I opened my own salon and from there I did hair up until 2006. Then I moved into the marketing brand and management for talent of YSquare Management.

Anything Yolanda wants, she can get.

—Artis Webb

Arriving from a positive environment is unique for an African American family. Because of the struggle, sometimes we do not get that. However, my dad was always positive. Therefore, he provided acronyms to keep us pumped, committed, and positive (PCP)! Because he started at such an early age, he was always inspiring. We were his first recruits. He tested his positive messages on us, no doubt believing, if he could motivate us to develop a positive frame of mind, he could do this business and inspire customers. My father did not come from a strong and positive environment. He came from a broken home. Thus, he had to become the leader in his family. Therefore, for him, to have a family, instill those types of qualities and always be positive—this stayed with us. Even now when we go through stuff and even when we feel crazy, we strive to find the positive side of CRAZY.

The legacy Dad taught me is entrepreneurism. I believe it is important as African American families to provide men with choices. The same way they are accustomed to living a wealthy life, I show them the skills required to build a business that helps one become self-sufficient. My son is an entertainer; he dances and sings, a fifteen-year-old and a four-year-old. Therefore, he is in the entertainment business. My husband is a national comedian, I manage him. Because I do brand management and entertainment production, my son observed his father changed from one level to the next. I saw the same transition with my father. Thus, the third generation is able to witness the same. In any kind of business relationships, the connection leads to other opportunities. Instead of waiting for someone to hand something to them or determining what jobs are available, my children are equipped to create opportunity for themselves. My kids know they can go out and create their own business. "We will get support the same way as our parents supported us." In addition, if they want to expand to another business as I did (knowing Kirby was a huge influence), they will do it! My husband also benefited from the positive influence of Dad!

Tone-X Belser, Mr. Webb's Son-in-Law

Mr. Webb makes you see life through a different telescope.
You're motivated to look at everything from a positive angle.

—*Tone-X Belser*

Comedy comes natural to Tone-X. His *WHY* for doing comedy is, "We all need to laugh." Shortly after returning from the military, Tone-X started working in comedy. At the age of twenty, he entered an "open mike" comedy contest in North Carolina. During this session, he met Walter Latham (Kings and Queens of Comedy). Over the next two and a half years, he would deliver spot tours with Chris Tucker, Bernie Mac, and Steve Harvey. During those twenty-five tours, comedians bounced off one another. This taught Tone-X a wealth about the comedy business. In 1995, Tone-X entered television via *Def Comedy Jam*. He moved on to complete three seasons of *Comic View* and *Bad Boys* comedy on HBO. Later he hosted Charlotte's no. 1 radio show, *Power 98*. About this time, Tone-X met Yolanda Webb. She came to visit the show one night. Her walk impressed him from a distance. He extended her a note to meet him after the show. He knew if she agreed to do so, it was a wrap. Today sixteen years later, they are married with children.

Meeting Yolanda automatically engaged her father Artis Webb. Tone-X is impressed with Artis Webb because he is a very positive individual. As the saying goes, association brings on simulation. The more you are around men like Artis Webb, the greater extent you will grow. Mr. Artis Webb makes you see life through a different telescope. You are motivated to look at everything from a positive angle. He always has good words to share . . . and he is just a good person to have around and reference to have in your life.

Young men . . . are looking for a hero (role model) to change the greatness within them. Here is where Mr. Webb delivers.

—*Tone-X Belser*

Tone-X believes Artis Webb's synergy is so unique for the African American community, because our home structures were destroyed. We are following a blueprint from someone else. In the past, the man was in charge of the family. Thus, all influence came from the man. Until, the single mom came first and man became secondary. A woman can raise a boy, but not a man . . . only insight from a female's point of view. Females get a right and direct model blueprint from their fathers. They can see the love Father has for Mother. Young men need to find people whom they can relate to, and most of the time, they are not your typical role model. They are really looking for a hero to bring out the greatness within them. Here is where Mr. Webb delivers. I think that his level of influence is still necessary in the African American community. We are a very spiritual people, because we are motivated by faith. Often we are not told that we are important. People may not express a genuine interest in us. We need to have more people like Mr. Webb, with words running prevalent. Artis delivers this level of dialogue and value in a large way. When people talk with him, they receive a positive attitude that he generates. This is something new for many people. The outcomes can change a mind-set, vision, and LIFE! I shared a wealth of conversations with Mr. Webb about the different aspects and guiding principles for a successful life. As demonstrated in the field of comedy, Mr. Webb considers relevant instances and communicates these via the lost art of conversation. A world of texting to communicate can leave emotion out of the conversation. I believe we need to try to understand other people. A telephone conversation appeals to all your senses, not just the sight as when reading a text. Mr. Webb delivers the art of conversation by providing positive energy. He deflates the negative and makes the conversation positive, a common ground, so we can relate and apply the principles. Personally, I credit much career growth to the many positive conversations and attitude adjustments developed while listening to my father-in-law, Mr. Webb. Today I enjoy tours with Monique and finishing branding a new book, *Grown Man Tips*. Because of Mr. Webb's influence, I enjoyed the honor of speaking at Kirby functions. For example, I can recall how some Kirby sales folks shared goals for the year, trips, and/or prizes they were looking forward to receiving. I shared, "If you are here to win a prize or chase money, you're in trouble. Because you are basing your life on what someone else is doing. If that is what you are doing, you are in for a rude awakening. You should remember to thank your wives and the family who is supporting you."

Tone-X believes this level of balance is important, because the business may end and retirement arrives, but you may not know the most prized asset—your family. Why? Because people often give everything to the business. Most of all, you have to love what you do and do what you love. Sometimes we will encounter people in businesses that are not genuine. However, if you live like Mr. Artis Webb and take a genuine interest in people, it is revealed in your life and a number of positive results. Artis believes you have to live what you say—tough angle. When you help other people implement positivity in their lives, then those same people will pay it forward and help others.

> *Just as he's had a good run with Kirby, I am hoping he can*
> *make the next run for himself and family.*

> —*Tone-X Belser*

As Mr. Webb has invested so much time and life in Kirby, I am hoping he understands there comes a time to walk away from the game. You can compare this to the boxer philosophy, "The boxer is still in you, so you may continue to fight after experiencing a successful career." In other words, when you can no longer be a boxer, teach others to fight. Thus, just as Mr. Webb enjoyed a good run with Kirby, I am hoping he can make the next run for himself by branching out into something different, beneficial, but on a much smaller scale than Kirby. I personally know he longs to enjoy more time to take advantage of his beautiful family structure. Thus, I see him delivering speech tours, writing more books, influencing positivity across the globe, and within that space, he will still be very powerful. In addition, skills as a top sales guru and business mogul will still shine through his children. One great example of sales leadership is his youngest daughter, Mehgan Webb. She is inspired by her dad and looks forward to breaking his sales records.

Mehgan Webb, Sales Manager

> *My dad became a factory distributor. He owns his business, he*
> *is self-sufficient; nobody can fire him. There's no salary cap.*
> *You can become a multimillionaire!*

> —*Mehgan Webb*

By providing leadership to my team, I strive to motivate others with inspiration. Daily sales meetings begin with passion, authentic thought leadership, and I leverage this team motivation in the field. My parents raised us to believe in family and to support each other, and whatever the mind can conceive, the body will achieve.

From Meghan, with Love and Appreciation!

I came along after my parents arrived to the good life. Thus, the lush life was normal for me. My dad is my hero! His perseverance and love for his family bolted his goal to support family. In addition, unlike his upbringing, he wanted to provide an opportunity to inherit something built for the family. Dad always taught me to not let a lack of confidence, race, or gender slow me down.

Mom taught me that a good man deserves a good woman to hold him down. In addition, the same woman should be courageous enough to let him know when he is wrong and be there to help him correct it. I have never feared for my parents' relationship or our livelihood. Through Kirby, my parents gave us a reason to be more than the average. In addition, they inspired us to drive beyond the limits of our minds. Thus, we strive to search within our hearts and live a life with passion and intent. I love my dad for setting such an amazing example and a powerful household. As a family, we are an invincible and unbreakable unit. My parents' legacy will live through their children. For example, I have set a goal to become a factory distributor by December. Thus, I look forward to accomplishing and achieving that goal, making my parents proud and exhibiting the same loyalty to parents as they have shown to us. Here is a little about how my dad's tutelage increased my knowledge and success in the Kirby business.

The Upbringing of Kirby Girl

We didn't know what it was like to be around people that didn't want to become successful entrepreneurs.

—*Mehgan Webb*

I came along after my parents arrived to the good life. Therefore, the lush life was normal for me. My dad was factory distributor (like a doctor of business). He has his own business. He is not responsible to anyone, has overall concessions to his business, set goals, and is self-sufficient; nobody can fire him. There is no salary cap. You can become a multimillionaire. For example, Leon Thomas (top distributor in the world) lives in a country club home (recruited, trained, and promoted by Mr. Webb); he sold eighty-thousand-plus Kirbys in the business over the last twenty-eight years. Such sales leaders have a locker next to Michael Jordan at the country club. The potential is limitless. We always enjoyed great things and environments filled with successful people. Thus, we did not know what it was like to be around people that did not want to become successful entrepreneurs. He was a celebrity to me, because he became national sales manager when I was four and we moved to Ohio. Everywhere he went, people flocked and went crazy around him. I never understood what he did. However, he was on that stage, giving his heart and soul. People would just flock over him. The words he shared with us on a personal level were always so positive. Just as he shared with Yolanda, he shared with me: "Whatever Meghan wants, she gets." And he made it come true. We never asked for anything we did not receive. I enjoyed watching him work. Mr. Gene Windfeldt (former president and greatest president and factory distributor Kirby ever had) would often take me to the factory. He is so world-renowned that *Forbes* magazine wrote an article about Mr. Windfeldt. I was always around him. He always inspired me. In fact, I can remember when Dad traveled to over seventy different countries. I enjoyed it. Therefore, as I got older, it became a natural. "I am supposed to do Kirby." My brother AJ does Kirby. I was impressed with him, and he is special to me because he learned the business from another amazing distributor (Dave Urban). AJ learned the business from a different leader in Kirby. Therefore, he learned some skills through tough grit on his own. Therefore, I was always impressed how my brother was willing to do that.

> *Come what may, we always . . . support each other. Even when*
> *we don't have something, we never allow anyone to fail.*
>
> —*Mehgan Webb*

Being raised in a positive environment is unique. Today many will find a common thread for families and individuals to turn against each other. Even if you go on social media, you will find people who do not even trust their families. Come what may, we always stick together and support each other. Even when we do not have something, we never allow anyone to fail. We pick up my brother, sisters, and Mom with love. It is a natural survival and commitment to sustaining our families. That is the pattern and family ethic I was taught. When I was little, people were attracted to Dad because he was positive.

Inspiring the Third Generation

My legacy is "I am a Kirby girl." I changed from district to home school to learn Kirby at the age of sixteen. In August 2014, I will open my own office. My sales' vision includes a goal to build the next Artis, Aaron, Aj and Yolanda through my daughter Mya and Cj because the third generation has so many musical people. Thus, I want to help them develop their natural talents. If due to some unforeseen circumstance I died tonight, I want my kids to look back and say the same positive things I say about my mom and dad, such as "My mom is a hard worker. She took really good care of me, and illuminated choices." I want to become the next Artis Webb in high heels. I will break all his records. Added to this, I will become the next Leon Thomas in the family, who was promoted and went out twenty-eight years ago. I want to make my dad proud, show him all the things he taught me, and demonstrate that time and tutelage mean something to me. *From Meghan, with love and appreciation!*

Aaron Webb, Firefighter for the City of Charlotte

The Kirby business is not for the fainthearted.

—*Aaron Webb*

Since 2001, Aaron Webb has served as a firefighter for the city of Charlotte. In his spare time, he helps remodel homes. In addition, when time permits, he delivers service as an EMT support to a movie set. He confirmed:

> The Kirby business is not for the fainthearted. The business requires hard work . . . sales folks will receive more no(s) than yes. Most people do not want to live their lives that way. However, the payoff proves very profitable and quickly. So it takes much invested hard work to move through those reactions to success.

Aaron watched his father work ten to twelve hours a day for virtually a lifetime. He said, "Dad led by example!" Sometimes people took advantage of Dad. However, his response to these experiences was never bitterness. He always set the example as a leader in word and deed. This unbreakable quality is necessary in Kirby. Because it is not physical factors that make people quit Kirby; it is the lack of mental toughness. Thus, any salesperson arriving to this business needs to exhibit the Head Rhino's characteristics of mental toughness, regardless of the battle. The legacy of a strong work ethic and leading by example are invaluable gifts that I will always cherish from Dad.

Family is very important to us! Dad and I speak on a weekly basis. I never say good-bye without telling him how much I love him. In addition, Mom is still a valuable financial resource. When I encounter important decisions, I always run these through Mom. I trust and value my parents' opinions. Thus, it is best to involve those who have your back for big decisions. Therefore, whenever I face tough financial decisions, I always turn to her to explore the resources and options available, and of course, she leaves it up to me to choose the path of choice. During my growing years, we always had at least one family member staying with us. We would not miss a year without attending reunions on both sides. In fact, one thing I struggled with as a son is remembering when the economy got bad. I felt guilty or torn between the decision to remain a firefighter or depart to support my family. I knew how much Kirby meant to Dad. Thus, my appreciation goes out to AJ and Mehgan for staying on board to provide leadership, sales expertise, and people development and to contribute their personal legacies of talents to the business.

Growing up within a positive home environment was another unique experience. A wealth of African American friends experienced just the opposite within homes. Mom and Dad gave daily commitments to nurture a positive home environment. As a young person, sometimes it is hard to process what parents are trying to create for their children, the next generation. Now that I am older, I appreciate even more so Dad's willingness to build a foundation for his family. He worked hard in Kirby because he wanted to create a great legacy for family and a succession plan for our family. As I have grown older, Dad and I have become even closer friends. Mostly, I am proud of Dad for his hard work and for looking far in advance to provide a better life for his family. Sometimes families leave it up to children to fend for themselves.

Dad desired a greater legacy and endgame for the next generation. My hope for Mom and Dad is to see them transition into a less-hurried pace. In addition, to become a little more selfish to pursue some personal goals, aspirations, and contribution in the community. Seeing Mom and Dad do whatever makes them happy outside of work would be a great reward for me. Dad has given enough of himself to everyone else. Now it is time to be a little selfish for him and Mom. *"Love you, Mom and Dad!"*—*Aaron*

A. J. Webb, Distributor

Not until Dad arrived to my school for career day did I realize he raised us on a different and more positive level. Dad drove around town with a gray Mercedes and developed the reputation as the "Kirby Man." During school, peers approached me and said, "Hey, my parents work for your dad!" In addition to the inspirational training and example of Dad, I was honored to be trained by various people in Kirby. Sometimes African American families inherit wealth, but not very often do we give back to the next generation. My way of paying this appreciation forward includes helping the next generation of sales leaders achieve success. Dad always encouraged us to exceed his sales accomplishments. This would be a great way to demonstrate how much I learned from his incredible example. Dad always says his achievements can be compared to a journey through the alphabet. Thus, why not pick up where Dad left off? Setting a goal to exceed his records was always a topic of conversation to build the Webb family succession plan. Dad always discussed this succession plan for the family. My desire is to pass on the knowledge that others were kind enough to bestow upon me.

As my brother Aaron mentioned, I did not always understand why Dad worked so long or what my parents were trying to build for us. In fact, I remember Dad arriving home just before we turned in for bed. We would run downstairs and yell, "DADDY!" In addition, we would watch him fall asleep on the couch and play tricks on him. Dad created fun by including us in a wealth of phenomenal trips to beaches, mountains, and different places! Thus, I am so thankful to have two parents who work hard and still give their best because they want us to achieve a greater degree of success in the business.

Kirby is my future! I was raised to be a leader, entrepreneur, and own my own business. Having received this rite of passage from Dad, this is my legacy. I like the fact that not everyone can do Kirby. This makes the business more authentic. Leaders who succeed in this business are even more original. Most of all, I want my parents to increase their happiness. People live longer when they are investing lives into hobbies and other passions. They did a good job building a passion and a great foundation at Kirby. Now, I would like to see them enjoy some other aspects of life. Both are great givers. Therefore, my hope is for them to move away from focusing on the business and increasing investment in other important passions and priorities such as community, travel, congregation, consulting, etc.

Never will I forget the mental toughness demonstrated and instilled by my parents. You do not come across people that tough. Instead of talking philosophy, they created a legacy, developed us, and shared the credit. The standard and challenge they have established for me is to always be willing to push myself beyond the comfort zone. Therefore, like Dad, I can do what is required to build my family. My parents were willing to lose it all to build a foundation to support their family. Mom, thanks for being so close to us. When Dad was at work, she invested more time to take us shopping, performed as a disciplinarian, showered us with toys, and adopted our friends too. Mom has a tremendous amount of affection. For example, she would give me a kiss. Then I would wipe it off. Then she would just give another, insisting, "You're going to get some love again."

Dad, thanks for your investment of hard work. Again, I appreciate how you adopted a vision for your family and became very decisive a long time ago. You were determined that your family would not struggle as you did growing up. Dad grew up in a single-parent home with siblings and cousins. Therefore, he mostly had to fend for himself. Thus, when we needed sound advice, Dad always provided this, and from a good place. He always wanted his kids to be honest with him. He believed answers should not be predicated by our attitude, but we need to be firm about yes or no. Either way, he taught us to never wear our emotions on our sleeves. Always execute with the mental toughness inherited from the Head Rhino. This same quality enables me to remain determined and tenacious in building a successful sales business today. *"Thank you, Mom and Dad, for being so responsible, working hard to build a great career, foundation, and means for us to support our families."*—A. J. Webb

Delores Satterfield, Esquire, Sister-in-Law

Artis always had a great smile!

—Delores Satterfield

Artis and I shared similar backgrounds. For example, we both arrived from large families. This common trait made Delores feel comfortable around Artis. His family was large, and he always thought her family was loved. Like Artis, Delores spent years in the air force so she could go to college. This funding gave her an opportunity to travel. Thus, Delores spent time in Hawaii and went to law school, and now as a retiree, she enjoys working on property development projects—things she wants to do. Meeting Artis Webb invited her on a new path of learning. Although well traveled and preparing to go to law school, working as a dealer for Kirby helped her earn an income to pay for her first car. Delores admired Artis's professionalism and people skills. He is an outstanding negotiator. In addition, Artis knows how to place customers at ease, make them feel comfortable, endearing, and he makes people laugh. It is hard to depart from Artis without gaining a lesson in wisdom framed into an acronym or two. She confirms she cannot remember them all. However, she will never forget his strong set of social skills and sincere interest in people. As Artis was very sharp and equipped with outstanding salesmanship, she was confident that he could sell anything. Therefore, she was ready to learn from this guru. Thus, she signed up, ready to knock it out. Sometimes she brought her baby brother as an assistant. He would carry the Kirby. Delores knows you have to become a whole person to endure and evolve in sales like Artis. He has a special knack for challenging a sales force to learn from each sell. Whether they closed a sale or not, she still learned something and developed. Turn every experience into a positive by sharing what you learned with fellow colleagues. Therefore, he really stands out as a sales development leader. Once, Delores was so proud of herself because she sold a cash sale and for her, it was hard to do. Later the person decided to withdraw from the sale. Even still, Artis honored her for the skills delivered in closing the sale. By doing so, he taught her to turn a negative into something positive.

Delores continues to live by this philosophy today. Thus, anyone that benefits from the Webb-based learning process will learn how to turn a negative into a positive. My hope is that Artis will continue to be a mentor and take one or two people—young males in the family—show them, treat them, and articulate to them what it means to be a man. Sometimes we start out with a certain idea, stamina, but if we do not endure with tenacity, we will not remain standing nor achieve our goals or dreams in life. I am very proud of Artis, and I believe success should be measured in terms of things you know and apply and do consistently. Within a space, Artis is most definitely the champion. *"Thank you for grooming me, cheering me on, and for making my sister happy as an outstanding husband and example!"—Delores*

Tonie Webb, Artis's Younger Brother

For over twenty-seven years, Tonie Webb has served as a captain for a fire department. Added to these achievements, he is married to a very successful wife, the president and founder of CertusBank. She and three other people started the bank. However, interesting enough, for some portion of their lives, both worked for and supported Artis Webb as a dealer or office assistant. However, Tonie's admiration and relationship goes back forty-five years. As a child, Tonie remembers Artis's regular visits. When Tonie was ten years of age, Artis made it his custom to invite Tonie to spend summers with his family. He always looked forward to the visit. They did not treat him like a distant relative but like one of their sons. Christine called him her little son. Thus, they created a great journey for him and left a positive impression.

> *Artis and Christine provided me with clothes like*
> *I was one of their kids.*
>
> *—Tonie Webb*

After Artis left the air force, he chose one company to invest his talents: Kirby. The office was a place for Tonie to hang out. Tonie will never forget how unique his upbringing became because he had a positive big brother to be around. Artis and Christine were such great givers. They provided Tonie with clothes as if he were one of the kids. Tonie always returned home with new clothes and motivation to arrive at school, because as Tonie shared, "I was clean!" Considering Artis's and Tonie's background, positivity did not come easy. Both worked in the fields and had to contend with a host of other struggles. Therefore, anything Artis or Christine could do to create a different environment and positive role-model influence, they both did that. Artis not only provided a great environment but also became a spiritual mentor, helping Tonie see the value of applying Bible principles in his life.

As someone younger, he always looked at his older brother Artis to help him develop values and character. Even though Artis continued to grow and travel with Kirby, he always made sure we had spiritual mentors to help us become grounded spiritually and have positive focus on life. Artis also maintained a gift of placing you in the best position to leverage your talents. For example, when Tonie spent time at the office, Artis noticed his interests were in repair work. Thus, Artis showed him how to repair Kirbys, run errands, and assist in the repair center. Tonie was able to travel with Artis as he delivered presentations, made repair works—there was always something to do.

Within Tonie's current profession, he applied wisdom gained while working with Artis. For example, Artis always shared one of his favorite quotes: "A person convinced against his will is of the same mind still." Thus, if your mind is made up, no matter what one may share, you are still of the same opinion. This stayed with Tonie. He remembers this wisdom when counseling people today. Artis even provided Tonie funding to complete his bachelor's degree in industrial engineering. However, his only requirement was for Tonie to commit to four years. Added to this, Artis did not want Tonie to worry about Mom. Therefore, when she needed assistance, he came through: brought her a house. Although Artis may not realize it, he contributed a great deal to our family.

Tonie's hope for Artis is for him to become a positive motivational speaker. If he can find his niche in the speaking arena, he will have something to offer them. Tonie watched Artis motivate people at crowds. Thus, it would be a natural transition for him to share his talents as an impromptu speaker for Kirby and the sale forces. Tonie was always amazed by his plethora of quick thinking, great illustrations, humor, and acronyms. Back in the day, he listened to motivational speakers like Zig Ziglar. He was always listening to positive speakers. He knew what it takes in sales to motivate people. Thus, he has a huge amount of wisdom to share with the emerging sales leaders of tomorrow. *"Thank you, brother, for engaging, inspiring, and serving as a positive role model for me."—Tonie Webb*

Lance Casper, former 100+ Sales Dealer

"Artis taught me how to overcome adversity and remain unstoppable. Moreover, his values of career, family, and spirituality first, impressed me!"

—Lance Casper

I'd heard about Artis & Christine soon after I joined Kirby Part-time. I met them thirty years ago when I was an area distributor just starting to write some number, however they were running a 200+ Distributorship – yet they treated me like a peer. They were selling impressive volumes and promoting people but what impressed me the most about them was the balance they had in their life. Artis & Christine were going after success but they realized focusing on and succeeding in just one area of your life isn't true success. They also had a spiritual side and placed great emphasis on their children. Their business was thriving and they also had an outstanding reputation in the community.

Thirty years later, after getting to know each other very well, my opinion of them is higher. When Artis was National Sales Manager he met every member of my family and they felt the same way about him as I do. Once when Artis & Christine were in town for another Division's VIP Pro Club, they heard my mother was sick and made a special effort to go see her and spend time with her before she passed away two-months later. That visit meant the world to her and it showed me what I already knew, this was a couple of great character and integrity that have their priorities in life figured out.

Webb-Based Science Reflective Effective Audit

The Webb family followed Artis's example to the letter. In addition, the business became successful because of a pattern of focus, family ethic of support, and unity. Take a moment and jot down some ways you can instill this commitment and synergy within your own family. What approaches will you embrace to increase and sustain a positive legacy for YOUR sales career and family? How will they remember you?

1.

2.

3.

PART II

Self-Management:
Breaking Free from the
Addiction to Failure

Discipline is a personal decision. There are several types of discipline. Some people need to be shown how to discipline themselves. Therefore, you show them by example. A Native American proverb shared, "Tell me and I will forget. Show me and I may remember. Involve me and I will understand" and develop. This process leads to discipline development. An example is when you coach new recruits and they do not develop as rapidly. Self-discipline is when you arrive to the point of believing, "I can do it all by myself," showing you are teachable. You can perform when you want to, and execute that way all the time. Because you made a commitment and decided, "This is what I am going to do!"

The word *discipline* is synonymous with the word *disciple*, meaning "to train, teach beliefs in the thoughts and teachings of a leader." So you can see how a person who is disciplined can become successful. Something deep inside says, "My family and I deserve the BEST that life has to offer, not necessarily the best materially, but the *best quality* of life." Focus starts on the inside. Finally, discipline is being (1) self-motivated, (2) self-sufficient, and (3) most of all, self-enduring until the task is complete. How do you represent yourself? Consider the following:

What Statements Define Me?	
• *A birth certificate shows you were <u>born.</u>*	• *A driver's license shows you can <u>drive.</u>*
• *A death certificate shows you have <u>died.</u>*	• *A positive attitude shows you <u>believe.</u>*
• *A photo album shows you have <u>lived.</u>*	• *To believe shows you can <u>succeed.</u>*
• *A passport shows you have <u>traveled.</u>*	

The Goal
To believe shows you can <u>succeed.</u>
To succeed shows you can <u>lead.</u>
To lead shows YOUR greatness and <u>deed.</u>

The bottom line is YOU <u>represent</u> your character, your <u>core values</u>, and most importantly, the person <u>you are</u>!

> *Your only competition is self. Compete against yourself,*
> *become better, and always win.*

> —*Mulah Truth*

Self-discipline begins with striving to become a peak performer. This is the quickest way to embark on a personal quest to focus for excellence! Why? Because you are constantly alone with self. Therefore, focus on self-improvement. People have often asked how I was able to rebound from so many blows. I always responded, "C-O-M-P-E-T-I-T-I-O-N!" Yes, the struggle for the same objective. Competition has made many of my dreams come true. This quality revealed the competencies of self-discipline, desire, dedication, determination—the required tools when building on a dream. Through competition, I discovered who I am and who I am not. This skill gave me energy to fight when I was challenged. Thus, it taught me to be strong when faced with others much stronger. I learned to believe in my heart, that there is <u>NOTHING</u> I cannot do or accomplish in life!

Whether you win or lose, if you compete fairly and believe that you gave your best, YOU ARE a winner! Competition is my friend. It will not betray me because I will not betray myself. There must always be a reason for competition, and for me, that reason is that I love it! Competition is part of my survival. We are all in the same race, competing for survival in a world that keeps changing the rules. Equality has been the prize I have been competing for all my life. An equal share of everything is available for everyone. Until there is equality, I will compete for the rest of my life.

Finally, concentrated on making positive efforts toward inside tasks instead of outside negatives—competition! Competition! Competition!

Discipline Becomes Evident on the Outside

Self-disciplined sales leaders operate with or without the presence of managers. A typical business structure charges all power to direct the business decisions to higher-ups and less freedom of choices to others throughout the business. However, self-disciplined team members lead and understand the perspective on how to manage the sales daily and to do the things that are necessary for success. These necessary things include a minimum of three presentations a day, fifteen presentations per week, and sixty presentations per month. Self-disciplined managers and leaders also include remembering what brought them into the business. In addition, inspiring their team to remember the bottom-line reasons they arrived to the business: opportunity, family, obligations, and a desire to develop more than they were after doing the business.

Fifteen Reasons that Inspire People to Sell Kirbys

1. The opportunity vs. job
2. The product vs. versatility of uses
3. The big picture vs. examples of success
4. The convictions and enthusiasm of the trainer
5. The distributor's encouragement and success stories
6. Distributors' validation of you, your story, your success, and his or her vision for the company
7. An example from the sales clinic that developed amazing opportunities
8. Maintaining high intensity through the training
9. Fun training, fun racing, excitement, and competition among the groups
10. Being observant, knowing the mental and emotional appearance of people, not just the physical aspects
11. Loud voice modulation and projection
12. Follow-up and follow-through
13. Discernment of when you need reinforcement and assistance
14. Learning from the experiences around you
15. A continued humility and eagerness to refine your skills

We deliver a culture of aspiration that begins
with YOUR vision.

—*Artis Webb*

So what is your reason to manage and harness your personal POWER, INTERNAL FORTITUDE, and THE WILL to sell? Pick a number, embrace it, and execute sales success today! Another way we will rally your talents is during our daily sales clinics. Here is why you are going to be inspired to embrace the discipline of a self-disciplined sales leader.

Ask a person what comes first, vision or thoughts. People have to have a vision. One proverb shared, "A person without a vision will perish." Further, Goethe once said, "If you treat a person as they appear to be, you'll make them worse. However, if you treat a person as if they were what they potentially are, you'll develop them into what they can be." So if we treat team members as they CAN BE, they will DEVELOP into all they can possibly become. Most people have a low self-image. They base their self-image on how someone else respects or perceives them. They have a low self-worth based on the level of how much they respect themselves. Discipline requires you to own that yourself. This is why our backgrounds and environments correlate to a mentally conditioned attitude when people reason, "Maybe I don't deserve it?" Intuitively, we want to become better. We have to get into the right environment or create it.

Inside of us there's greatness, a sleeping giant
waiting to come alive!

—Tony Robbins

We have to awaken the sleeping giant inside (Tony Robbins). For example, you have 100 trillion cells. After you involve these 100 trillion cells, think about your abilities—you will become awe-inspiring! At this point, you will not believe there is a limit to what you can do. I don't think there are any mental limitations. HOPE (help other people excel) is an inspirational hallmark behind Kirby. Sometimes the hall of Kirby receives people who have given up on themselves. Their families have given up on them. They are homeless "mentally," in a sense that they can't see a way out of their circumstances. Physically, they have a place to live, but they cannot see themselves ever getting out of their situation. Always remember, your "present circumstances do not determine where you CAN GO; they merely determine where you START" (Nido Qubein).

Therefore, our educational and inspirational clinics help team members gain sales skills and an internal fortitude to create success in the field. Hal Lindsey helps us to appreciate the value of hope with these words (taken to the extreme): "Man can live about forty days without food, about three days without water, about eight minutes without air . . . but only for one second without hope." Without hope, people lack motivation to achieve goals to appreciate the value of life, and in some cases, once people give up hope, they give up on themselves and life in general. Therefore, every morning, we inspire our team members with the HOPE of champions they can and will become:

Help	Other	People	Excel

Sometimes new recruits share, "I don't care if I do well or not. I just need to feel better about myself. I don't have skills. I am shy and very bashful." Although recruits want to get out in the field, they look forward to clinics because this environment inspires a culture of aspiration and provides opportunities to sharpen their sales skills gained during each session. Within many educational circles, sales folks would have to pay fees to gain access to this high level of knowledge via workshops. However, we provide these sessions FREE of charge, because we believe if you send recruits out without skills, the probability of frustration runs high. Leaders need to inspire and breathe life into sales forces by using CPR (communicating positive, and reinforcement). This gives a sales team enough power to sustain themselves throughout the day. Placing a new sales force in the field without fortifying them is like placing a person in deep water without a life preserver. During morning sales meetings, we teach the seven basic principles for success in any endeavor. Success is a journey, and it should be pursued from the top down, not from the bottom up.

SEVEN STEPS TO SUCCESS

1. *Knowledge* of yourself, product, people, programs, and company
    (creates)
2. *Confidence* in yourself, product, people, programs, and company
    (creates)
3. *Enthusiasm* in yourself, product, people, programs, and company
    The last for letters in enthusiasm (*IASM*) means "I AM SOLD MYSELF!"
    (creates)
4. *Ability* to sell yourself, product, people, programs, and company
    (creates)
5. *Motivation* about yourself, product, people, programs, and company
    (creates)
6. *Volume* for your sales product, people, programs, company, and people
    (creates)
7. *Success* for yourself, product, people, programs, company, and others

In $UCCE$$, you have dollars and cents (U) + (E)arn the right to be successful! Earn those dollars and cents (U) and (E). SELL means SEE the customer, EXCITE the customer, LOVE the customer, and LEAVE the product. Serve the customer to the greatest degree possible.

Webb-Based Science Reflective Effective Audit

As an individual contributor, what will you do today to awaken the internal "sleeping giant of greatness" (Robbins, Year)? How will you develop as a sales leader and cultivate internal potential to lead?

1.

2.

3.

CHAPTER 4

Sales Strategy #1: Attitude

One of the most important qualities for self-discipline and success is attitude. This quality will determine your success. As I have traveled around the world with Kirby, successful leaders always possess a PMA (positive mental attitude). Sales are businesses about people. In order for us to become successful salespeople, we must master the art of dealing with people; we have to first understand them. It has been estimated that more than 22 billion people have lived and died on this earth. At present, we have over eight billion people living today. We have over eight billion people with three personality types. What motivates these people? Well, you have to perceive people from three categories.

The Wonderers, Watchers, and Innovators (or Makers)

- **Eighty-five percent belong to the "wondering generation" personality type**. This group exhibits the three *C*s (criticize, condemn, and complain). They always find something negative to say to everyone they meet. No doubt, you have met people like this. I hope that this is not your personality. Many walk around with a frown of disillusionment. It's been said it takes seventy-two muscles to frown and only fourteen to smile. Therefore, you can imagine the pressure this person has on himself when they manifest this type of attitude. They believe the world owes them something. They are very despondent. You probably know someone like that personally or intimately. It has been said, "The best thing they can do is brighten up the room by leaving it." Eighty-five percent is a great number. Therefore, it is important to not manifest this attitude. They are a part of a wondering generation that goes through life wondering what happened.

- **Thirteen percent belong to the "watching generation" personality type.** They predicate their success on the success of other people. They mirror and draw strength from other people. They mirror the environment they are in. They have been referred to as "a two-faced person," comparable to an adjustable wrench that is always trying to find some nut to adjust to. They mirror their environments. In the words of Zig Ziglar, they are referred to as SNIOPs (susceptible to the negative influence of other people) or PPIOOPs (perceptive, positive influence on other people). These remind me of myself when I first came to Kirby. I was not positive or negative; I had FUDS (fearful, uncertain, doubtful, and skeptical). With negative people, they influence you in negative ways. With positive people, they influence you in positive ways. If you are part of this group, you have to associate with people who want to go forward in the sales business. When you do that, your success is assured to you.

- **Two percent belong to a "league of innovators."** These people make things happen! This group will always commend, encourage, and are positive. Less than 2 percent commend people; they are positive, look for the good in others, and always encouraging someone. So think about it. Less than 2 percent of people in the richest nation in the world earn a six-figure income. These people want something out of life. They make it happen and realize, "If it's going to be, it's up to me!" So this group works against the negative machinations and work through the distractive forces. They do not necessarily want to sell but believe that is the only option for ultimate success. This group of innovators is easy to spot because they are always positive. They go the extra mile and deliver a 100 percent effort. At all times this group continues to commend, encourage, and give positive vibes, and they always put forth an extra effort even if the outcome is not what they expect.

What Can We Focus On to Become a Part of the 2 Percent Club?

1. **Develop good work habits**. Market a minimum of three presentations a day and fifteen per week. In other words, do whatever you can to deliver success.

2. **Become self-sufficient**. Generate your own lead leads. Avoid wasting time sitting around waiting for appointments from the office of others.

3. **Exercise discipline**. Do not shortcut your presentations or value to the customer. Allow customers the opportunity to see the full value of the Kirby or whatever product you are selling. Go the extra mile!

> *Discipline [defined]: doing what you have to do, and doing it*
> *as well as you possibly can, and doing it that way all the time.*

> —*Robert Knight, Hall of Fame Basketball Coach*

Remember, it is not so much what you are doing in Kirby compared to what you are becoming in Kirby (or within any sales career). We are equipped with the freedom of choice. Choose which group you want to belong to: wonderers, watchers, and innovators (and makers). Once you make the choice, then the choice controls you. If you want to become a member of the top 2 percent, start wherever you are today. The efforts you expend today will make a difference. Join me as we take the next step on your road to success.

Webb-Based Science Reflective Effective Audit

What percentile describes your attitude? Is it the 85 percent who wonder, criticize, and complain? The 13 percent who sit on the side and watch? The top 2 percent who FINISH what they start? What characteristics are keeping you from reaching goals? Are your influences negative, or positive? How can you become one of the top 2 percent? Jot down three things you will do today to become a part of the 2 percent group of FINISHERS!

1.

2.

3.

CHAPTER 5

Sales Strategy #2: Successful Thinking

Negativity cannot remain without a hook to hang on.
Positivity and happiness can be without any reason.

—*Sri Ravi Shankar*

During Webb's career, he was not willing to settle for second best. After earning his Five-Diamond Medallion and President's Pen in seven short months, he was promoted to field supervisor and made forty-five sales during his first month. Artis's team went on to top seventy-five sales each month thereafter, with a high month of 105 sales. As an area distributor or distributor trainee, he achieved 127 sales in one month. He worked hard to maintain his passion and enthusiasm. Thus, he positioned himself at the top of his division. As he continued to climb the ladder of success, he occupied the top positions, such as (a) no. 1 part-time dealer, (b) no. 1 dealer, (c) no. 1 field supervisor, (d) no. 1 area distributor or distributor trainee, and (e) no. 1 distributor in his division for a total of four straight years.

There is no way in the world you will convince me to leave a
professional engineering job to sell vacuum cleaners!
No way in the world!

—*Daryl Walker*

Daryl arrived at Kirby after working six years in corporate as a mechanical engineer and a graduate of Georgia Tech. He lived for the vision of one day becoming a principal engineer to lead engineering projects for his firm—a path that could lead to an annual salary of $200,000. If he could just stay focused and commit twenty-five more years to his engineering firm, his career goals would arrive. During this time, Daryl's fiancé worked for Kirby. As his goal was climbing the corporate ladder, it was no surprise for him to respond to his future wife's invitation to join Kirby with these words: "*There is no way in the world you will convince me to leave a professional engineering job to sell vacuum cleaners! No way in the world!*" Nevertheless, his future wife most certainly persuaded him to consider the possibilities of Kirby. During a return to Atlanta, he explored the Kirby opportunity. While working for his former distributor, he still refused to believe one could become successful and profitable by selling vacuum cleaners. Thus, his distributor decided to call Artis Webb and insisted, "I have this really sharp guy! Would you be willing to come down and talk with him?"

Mr. Webb arrived at a restaurant and spent some time getting to know Daryl. The outcome of this meeting led to an appointment at Mr. Webb's office. During this appointment, Artis said, "I am willing to take you out with me in the field. I am a divisional supervisor [an executive in Kirby similar to a vice president in corporate], and I am ready to show you how easy it is to excel in the Kirby business." Artis invited Daryl to lead him to a neighborhood that he considered prosperous. After Daryl located the neighborhood, Artis started knocking to demonstrate how easy it is to help people and deliver a great product. The first knock he engaged a wife alone. She insisted, "I've seen the Kirby before. In fact, someone presented the product about two months ago." However, Artis responded, "You have not seen this one." The woman added, "Oh, you have a new one?" Thereafter, the woman invited Artis and Daryl to present the product. Artis invited Daryl to "sit down, I am going to show this Kirby." So let us review the setting. Artis sat down with a woman who just saw the Kirby product two months ago and finished the paperwork. Later the husband arrived home, watched a few benefits and features of the Kirby product, and replied, "We should have bought this the first time." The former distributor actually presented the product two months ago.

Aside from Artis coming to the field to show a new dealer an easy process, the next move would also amaze and persuade Daryl. After the woman completed the sale, Artis looked at Daryl and said, "I need you to sign right here . . . this is YOUR FIRST SALE." Thereafter, sometime later, Daryl began working with Artis. In time, Artis promoted him out to the distributor he is today.

> *Mr. Webb works hard; he is filled with so much information*
> *and knowledge it is ridiculous, and he*
> *performed successfully.*

> —*Daryl Walker*

The life-changing moment arrived for Daryl when Mr. Webb, a divisional supervisor (a Kirby executive similar to a VP), demonstrated a willingness to roll up his sleeves and show him a transparent process that leads to success. Added to this, Artis demonstrated a behavior rarely exhibited in the sales leadership arena: he gave the sale to a new dealer. Based on Daryl's former career paths, most supervisors are not about to take anybody out to the field. However, Mr. Webb wanted Daryl to experience the joy and ease of working in the Kirby business without actually being in the business. Thus, it was a game changer to meet a divisional supervisor willing to make sacrifices to inspire and show a new dealer a simple process to arrive at success. This level of engagement from senior leaders is the key to success!

Daryl arrived from a traditional professional family. His father was an engineer, and his mom served as a schoolteacher. However, Kirby instilled a new paradigm shift. Because Daryl decided to accept Mr. Webb's invitation to join Kirby, he moved from a small apartment to a six-thousand-square-foot house on a golf course. Prior to Kirby, he was on a path to reach $200,000 a year with a time frame of twenty-five years. However, via Kirby, *he reached this financial goal within a shorter period.* In fact, within a few years, he earned more money than both his mom and dad combined.

Kirby is one of the greatest career secrets. Some know about Kirby. However, most information travels via word of mouth. Although Kirby offers success, one has to be willing to work hard, grind it out, and stay focused on success to excel in this industry. If you WORK IT, it will WORK! Kirby is relevant to a new culture and interesting economic climate. In the past, parents worked for one job, 9:00–5:00 p.m., and stayed there for life. Today, nine-five schedules with weekends off are from a time designed for dinosaurs. Today's companies are focused on the bottom line. For example, if my company is bringing in one million dollars per year, I am not going to pay you $900,000. This helps his team gain clarity regarding how much money is needed to pay bills, the amount actually coming in, and IF you cannot pay your bills. When one works from paycheck to paycheck, this person hopes nothing tears up in between or runs out. Nevertheless, some departed with the decision to become "a professional broke person."

Daryl learned that working by the hour like parents performed proved successful in the past. Our parents worked for and remained loyal to one company. Today the world has changed. Most employees no longer honor the "psychological relationship," which assures employees will have a job if they deliver great work. Today, it all boils down to the bottom line. For example, let's pretend my company provided me two options: (a) pay you fifteen dollars per hour to punch holes in this metal so you can have this car *or* (b) take it overseas and pay someone eight dollars (50 percent less) to make the same product. I am sorry; I will choose the path to help me increase my bottom line.

Today I am grateful to Mr. Webb for instilling a career intervention. IF Mr. Webb would have failed to show me how to become a success, I would still be on my ten-year trek, hoping and praying to maintain tenure and receive a future promotion in a right-to-work state. Mr. Webb works hard; he is filled with information . . . he has so many years of knowledge in him it is ridiculous, and he has performed successfully.

Thank you, Mr. Webb! Your career intervention and
investment with me in the field changed my life!

—Daryl Walker

The Secret to Successful Sales Thinking

To understand the secret, you have to understand your thought process. You must first understand the way your mind works. Your mind is like an iceberg. Visualize the part above water as the conscious part. According to MacGregory (2008) the conscious mind is estimated to be only 12 percent of our mind. However, the part with the greater impact is 88 percent. All unconscious thoughts contribute to building our unconscious mind. We gravitate into the direction of our most dominant thoughts. We cannot think positive and negative at the same time; we are either positive thinkers or negative thinkers.

For example, while giving a speech at a sales rally, I repeated these words (several times): "You become what you think about the most. You become what you think about the most." Then a person in the back of the room yelled, "Oh no, I am becoming a woman!" Obviously, his most dominant thoughts were on women. Here is another example. If I said, "Do not think about a big pink elephant or rhino with floppy ears, purple spots, and wearing sunglasses." What image would fill your mind? An image of an elephant or rhino, but not the word *rhino*! Because our minds see things in pictures, our subconscious mind cannot store a positive and negative thought at the same time. Did you know a negative thought stays in your unconscious mind for twelve to twenty-four hours? In addition, it takes six to twelve positive thoughts or affirmations to erase one negative thought. This is why you must challenge yourself to focus on a positive image of your future and visualize it as a reality. Always strive to work hard, focus on positive goals, and maintain a positive mental attitude. Here's how:

Positive Affirmations

This applies to any statement that makes you feel different or negative about you.

According to Jack Canfield, anytime you hear a negative comment such as

"You can't get in that door!" Tell yourself, *"Go for it anyway!"*

"No matter what you say or do to me, I am still a worthwhile person!"

"You can't sell Kirbys!" Tell yourself, *"Go for it anyway!"*

"No matter what you say or do to me, I am still a worthwhile person!"

"You can't make anything in Kirby!" Tell yourself, *"Go for it anyway!"*

"No matter what you say or do to me, I am still a worthwhile person!"

That is how you cancel out negative thoughts and reinforce positive thinking—by saying, "I am great and I like myself." Then you reinforce it by looking to the right or left, by saying, "You got that right!" Affirm this with someone next to you. Positive thinking works, because positive thinkers focus on what they want and naturally gravitate toward goals. When you do, you are building your own self-respect. You will always stand tall in your own mind through positive affirmations. Your subconscious mind contributes greatly to your success by improving and visualizing it through the eyes of faith. So start programming yourself for success. Such as "I will make at least two to three presentations today." Think, act positive, be positive, and say, "I will make one sale today!" or "I will do whatever necessary to complete the program and become a factory distributor or successful business owner or entrepreneur.

Webb-Based Science Reflective Effective Audit

How would you define yourself? Describe your reactions when faced with disappointments and criticisms? How many positive thoughts enter your mind each day? List your BEST qualities and interpersonal skills below. Write down a positive affirmation to refute negative thoughts. START applying positive thoughts about yourself today! You were meant to achieve greatness!

1.

2.

3.

CHAPTER 6

Sales Strategy #3:
Prepare to Value and Lead a Team

When you come in sales, you have to have a SELF-WORTH
beyond your NET WORTH that people place on
you when you go to a job.

—Artis Webb

Sales and leadership are not often stated in the same sentence. In the sales departments, it is assumed that team members are confident, successful, unstoppable, and maintain an unlimited amount of self-worth. The lack of confidence can be revealed in an overabundance of braggadocio rights to recognize self. However, sometimes people suffer from three things in sales and life:

- **Self-image.** They think this is the way other people see them. However, it is the way they see themselves. Your environment can dictate the health of your self-image.
- **Self-esteem**, the respect they have for themselves. Sometimes they do not have enough respect for themselves. They believe they have to present themselves in a way to be accepted by other people. They do not have the intuitive or high-standardized level of respect for self.
- **Self-worth**, the value you put on yourself. This is the understanding that there is no limit to what you can accomplish if you do not care who gets the credit. Whenever you accept an amount to work for, people generally attach this to their self-worth and extent of their work ability.

When you arrive to the field of sales, you have to have a self-worth beyond the net worth that people place upon you at a typical job. For example, a job may give you ten dollars per hour. Self-worth is when you can say, "I believe that I should not put limits on what I can do. I'd rather take the risk and go for a greater self-worth, without setting a limit on the minimum I can do." This will reflect my true value or a more accurate awareness of my authentic value.

During your first thirty days, invest time to first observe the teams' talents. Your role as a leader is to determine sales members' talents, strengths, weakness, and leverage talents to deliver team success. After thirty-one days, start using the TSW profile approach to assess strengths observed in your team. Perceive your team members' talents and career maturation via this lens. Your goal is to move them from good to great, from great to excellent, and from excellent to significant.

The TSW Talent Assessment Tool

Talents. After thirty days, observe your sales force and identify what talents come natural. On day thirty-one, take inventory of observations you have observed. What are their talents? What comes natural? Some people can sing. That is a talent or a gift. People who cannot sing will never be as good as a person who has a gift for it. You can train and teach yourself to sing. However, you will never be as good as the person who has a natural gift. Some people have a gift, which is their gift. Sometimes people arrive to Kirby with natural charisma, interpersonal skills, greet others, and add value to people. What talents did you observe in your sales team?

Strengths. If you have talent, do you support that by fortifying self to increase maximum operation? For example, Michael Jordan was excellent at basketball. However, he was disciplined; despite his wealth of athleticism, he allowed himself to be in excellent condition—mentally, physically, and emotionally—for the talent he had. Weaknesses always have a way of manifesting themselves. However, your weaknesses are controlled when you focus on your strengths.

Weaknesses. This measurement always has a way of manifesting itself. Sometimes a person's weakness is a more predominant quality than talents and strengths. Thus, it is incumbent upon you as a leader to search for their talents and strengths. You can acknowledge and ignite these talents to bring them out. When sales members can embrace their strengths, their weaknesses will not have a chance to overtake their gifts, talents, and abilities.

A sales department is the revenue that drives the business.

—*Artis Webb*

Naturally, two-thirds of us will succeed because we have talents and strengths. However, when our self-image, self-esteem, and self-worth are so low, these can overtake our success factors. For example, if we show up late, this is a weakness. Especially as a leader, we set the example for future sales leaders to follow. Thus, lead by example. When we lack focus, we are distracted. Therefore, we allow our weaknesses to overshadow any talents or strengths we may have. Everyone wants to be motivated! A sales department is the revenue that drives the business. Thus, it is critical that this league of leaders receives an effective model to follow, inspire, enhance, motivate, and leverage their strengths. Then they will feel and believe they are superstars! So never be afraid to address this dialogue in the very beginning. Make an effort to explore their strengths and talents. This discovery will help you take advantage and build sales managers of tomorrow. Therefore, first lead, then others can observe and learn by YOUR example.

Management vs. Leadership

We're all works in progress, honey. And believe me when I tell you that I've had to work harder than most.

—*Susan E. Phillips*

A manager is a person who wants to direct and tell others what to do. They seek the explicit details. However, they do not realize the example they set is greater than what they say. Alternatively, a leader is a person that influences and leads by example. They are leading and managing at the same time. You can manage and not lead, but it is difficult to lead and not manage. Your leadership, influence, charisma, and example inspire sales teams to taking note. In addition, your example manages and encourages them to derive some nuggets from your example. Although they may never deliver things on your level, with learning and time management, they can become like their leader!

Leon Thomas, Voted No. 1 Distributor in the World

One key to success is building an atmosphere of trust . . .
deliver what you claim . . . and pay people for
work rendered . . . keep it simple.

—Leon Thomas

During the last twenty years in Kirby, Leon purchased more Kirbys than any active Kirby distributor. In 2012 and 2013, he was voted no. 1 distributor in the world. Leon enjoyed the honor of being trained by Mr. Webb. He worked under Mr. Webb for four years. The greatest retention aspect of working for Mr. Webb was his honesty, strong values, and ability to create a family atmosphere. Leon was relieved to arrive to a company and culture he could trust. This workplace culture is critical to a successful business. One can find people who are skilled and talented. However, if these same leaders are unethical, their careers will prove unfulfilling. Therefore, Leon arrived to Kirby while still attending college as a major in civil engineering. Kirby was a way for him to make extra cash to invest in real estate. After the interview, Leon learned how a dealer could earn a range of 100–150 dollars every time they sold a Kirby. So his goal was to sell one or more Kirbys per week. After three weeks of working on a part-time basis for Kirby (and keeping one afternoon appointments per day), he discerned he was generating a higher income than the amount formerly earned in his full-time job as a civil engineer. Thus, he decided to work at Kirby full-time. The rest is history.

Like Mr. Webb, he agrees it is important to create an atmosphere of trust. Next, deliver what you promised to your team. Pay people for work rendered. Thus, living by a structure of an ethical business will eliminate problems in the forms of attitudes or retention of dealers. Added to ethical leadership, remember, "Sales run the business. Everything else is secondary. If you're selling the merchandise, buying more Kirbys, paying the people who sold, then you'll witness a repeat cycle of success. Therefore, keep things simple."

Leon is thankful to Mr. Webb because he gave him the opportunity he would have given anybody. He shared, "Thank you for the amount of knowledge you shared. By sharing your thought leadership, you increased my capacity of prior knowledge and gave me tools to create success in Kirby." As an avid reader of books, Mr. Webb is truly a lifelong learner. Therefore, Leon was able to benefit from his knowledge during sales meetings. The experience enhanced Leon's appetite for studying and team leadership. Because Mr. Webb shares his gifts of inspiration and care for people from the heart, Leon believes he would touch more people as a motivational speaker! Some successful people believe they cannot become as successful as their mentor can. However, Mr. Webb proved that the most effective mentor is willing to set the stage of what a salesperson can and will deliver in the future, for self and your sales team.

Thank you for investing in my growth and success and as a sales professional.

—*Leon Thomas*

Leaders will allow a sales force to use their own autonomy. They are working to become an entrepreneur. The risk is, they may fail. However, let them go ahead and develop a management style so they can get things accomplished. Even in the event of failure, the process enables them to develop a structure and management philosophy to lead with success.

Webb gives his sales force the autonomy to understand responsibility. When he notices they are not going into the direction they should be going, he gives them a life lesson or advice. We become great through the diversity and adversity of other people. That is why it is so important to apply a positive attitude, thinking, and vision to see your sales team's talents. In addition, coach and inspire them every day to become the leaders they are truly capable of achieving. You have to be willing to meet people where their hurt is. Thus, if you want to feel you are uplifting someone, determine where he or she is hurting—spiritually, emotionally, economically—and orient his or her most dominant focus. Artis was great, supporting the growth of team leaders and promoting business growth for other distributors.

Rich Rasner, Former Kirby Distributor and Supervisor

The odds of making it in Kirby are not very good.

—*Rich Rasner*

Rich knows about determination. When he started with Kirby, he missed his first seventy-seven presentations. Customers laughed him out of their houses. However, in time, he succeeded as a distributor. During the 1990s, he met Artis while he served as the national sales manager. To him, Artis maintained an *Action Jackson* style. Because sales rooms engage "a lot of talkers," an intentional approach to delivery is important. For example, some claim, "If I can put on one hundred presentations today in theory, they will be successful." Artis and Rich were the doers!

New York City was the location for one of Artis's greatest success stories! This location is one of the toughest markets in the world. Most people go bowling and bring the ball forward—in New York, they throw overhand. The story started after Artis delivered one of his fearless speeches. Artis encouraged this sales group: "You don't try, just go out there and make it happen!" In the audience was a saleswoman who needed one more sale to meet her goal for the month. The woman put on one more presentation in New York City after 9:00 p.m. After meeting with disappointment, she returned to the office and shared, "Surely the Head Rhino wouldn't be afraid at eleven p.m. in NYC!" Therefore, Artis accepted the challenge by rising up at 11:30 p.m. to knock on doors somewhere in New York City. Without surprise, Artis enters the car with this younger dealer. Next, he knocks on a door, puts on a presentation from 11:45 p.m. to 1:30 a.m., and closed the final sale in cash. After this tenacious delivery, Artis became larger than Superman!

Everybody in sales is either big boosters or detractors.
Artis was always a Rich Rasner's fan!

—*Rich Rasner*

Artis's strength as a positive influencer made a tremendous difference in Rasner's life. For example, Rich became a supervisor over Charlotte, North Carolina, and surrounding areas. Artis was a former distributor in this location for almost fifteen years. Rich's career was enriched from knowing the Webb family. Artis was formerly in Charlotte and now in Atlanta. Artis was supportive of Rich. Everybody in sales is either big boosters or detractors. Artis was always a Rich Rasner's fan. He watched Rich's transition from a great distributor to a divisional supervisor over North Carolina, Tennessee, and South Carolina. Therefore, when Rasner became a supervisor, Artis was like his assistant for his division in Charlotte. As Artis knew the culture and diversity of these dealers, he provided warm transfers and connections to help Rasner build great relationships in Charlotte and throughout his division. This assisted Rich with his team's effectiveness.

Everybody always said they broke the mold
when they made Artis.

—*Rich Rasner*

In support of Rich, Artis promoted him as an example and leader. Because of this company support, skill, and hard work, Rich's team succeeded in sales. Rich had a dream to become no. 1 distributor in the world. The top global distributor will provide a difference between one and five, another office, and forty more sales a month. During this campaign, Kirby was giving away a new Jaguar. Rich figured that if he just sell at least 850 Kirbys per month, he might qualify. His team planned a success strategy for almost one year. Well, he did not sell 850. *Instead his team sold 1,200 Kirbys in one month ($960,000 in one month).* It was like a dream come true for him and his incredible team! As a bonus, Rich was awarded the Jaguar because of such unprecedented sales success!

Artis is a standout person for inspiring others through his speeches. He always arrived as a speaker to deliver a grand-slam homerun. There are so many stories and so many trips we shared together. Artis always encouraged a positive attitude, enthusiasm, and whatever his theme most appropriate for his audience. He really has a passion for helping people succeed. In fact, one should be careful to avoid playing basketball with Artis. As he is committed to success, he is competitive on the field and aims to win. Therefore, now you can see why people always said, "They truly broke the mold when they made Artis!"

A little less than a decade ago, Rich left Kirby to pursue new opportunities, and he is remembered for his outstanding sales goal and earnings of $960,000 in one month for selling 1,200 Kirbys. He and his wife maintained friendships, affection, and appreciation for Artis and Christine Webb. Rich shares:

> *I can't tell you how proud I am to know Artis and Christine. I truly believe he would be a great motivational speaker or any other endeavor he chooses to pursue! After creating success in one of the most challenging markets of direct sales, I do not think there is anything Artis cannot deliver! Thank you for being a great supporter and encouraging friend! (Rich Rasner)*

Leadership is not a position; it is a way to influence future sales leaders of tomorrow. It is what you do, the qualities they see, and then inspiring them for what they want to BE! Remember, there are natural-born leaders that exhibit talents and strengths that are not taught. Nevertheless, there are those taught through information. This becomes knowledge, which develops into practical skill. Once implemented, it becomes your experience. As you refine it, this becomes a science. Then ultimately, you become the ARTIST of your own craft! You can perceive, visualize, and paint any picture of success you desire. Then it materializes into whatever material prosperity or success commodity you want it to be!

Webb-Based Science Reflective Effective Audit

What are your talents, strengths, and weaknesses? What did you discover about your team's talents during the first thirty days? Next, how will you leverage the team's talents to embrace this opportunity and shine as sales leaders? Write down the goals you have set to lead, cultivate, and nurture a phenomenal team.

1.

2.

3.

Part III

Management of Sales Teams

This business is 20 percent technical and
80 percent interpersonal.

—Artis Webb

In applying the 80/20 rule of business, 20 percent of salespersons earn 80 percent of the money. Added to these percentages are the 20 percent of people who do 80 percent of the work. Therefore, it should not surprise you to discover how we distribute profits. In addition, this structure helps you to complete early identification of leaders in the business. Artis experienced the 80/20 rule during his transition from sales dealer to corporate leader. The former vice president of corporate shared a special trust and bond with Artis. In addition, as a leader he shared some important unwritten rules required to manage and lead across the Kirby Corporation. Collectively, Artis and Marshall underscore the importance of honoring a diversity of talents.

Management Spotlight

Marshall Heron, Former Vice President of Kirby

Trust is something you have to earn . . . you need to trust us.

—Marshall Heron

Artis and Marshall worked together in Cleveland. Marshall was the VP of Kirby. Artis arrived as he was transitioning from dealer to corporate employee. This duo delivered distributor orientations together in Cleveland; seven hundred distributors developed through Cleveland. One reason for the success of their relationship is a special bond of trust. This quality is essential to any good business relationship. Both parties have to trust each other. The most successful relationships require time to develop. One day Artis asked Marshall, "When will you and Gene trust me to run my place and make my own decisions?" Marshall responded, "Trust is something you have to earn. Because you are new, we are watching to see what you will do. Trust takes time. In the meantime, you need to trust us." Artis thought this was terrific!

Transitioning from Dealer to a Corporate Executive

Marshall remembers the transition from the field of independent distributor to an employee for the Kirby Company. Mr. Gene Windfeldt and Marshall agreed it was fair to prepare Artis on his new role as a corporate employee and the culture so he would transition successfully. Both coached from their own unique experiences and growth in Kirby. Marshall told Artis, "Arriving to corporate requires a new level of thought leadership. Prior to this moment, you represented yourself. Now you represent the big picture, and YOU ARE the big picture. This role requires a new level of brand and company responsibility. Now you are looking for performance to make sure sales folks do and say the right things."

Artis matriculated quickly, lending to the good trusting relationship shared by him and Marshall. In fact, the best times in Kirby career were enjoyed when the team of Gene, Artis, and Marshall worked together. During this time, they sold a great many machines—two of the best years, back to back.

Trips to Europe, "Salt and Pepper"

The unique seasoning defined their unique speaking styles,
abilities, and successful impact on audiences.

—*Marshall Heron*

At one point, Artis and Marshall traveled together to Europe because both had a different way of communicating. Marshall believed, "Between the two of us, we'll get the job done!" Some may associate the nickname Salt and Pepper with Artis's race of African American and Marshall's race as a Caucasian male. However, the unique seasoning defined their *unique speaking styles, abilities, and successful impact on audiences.* Once, Artis and Marshall were charged to introduce a new product in Europe. Upon arrival, they would always meet big sales rallies. When they arrived to Brussels, Belgium, they discovered over one thousand people in attendance for that conference! Artis was ready to deliver his speech in his customary way of using acronyms and rhymes, talking fast, and watching people get excited and jump on their feet. Whether they understood or not, they will understand most and will stand on their feet cheering. Prior to his arrival to the stage, Marshall shared, "Artis, you know these people speak a different language. Sometimes they may not understand you. Sometimes I don't understand you because of your fast pace." Artis laughed, walked on stage, and forgot everything Marshall shared. After a few rhymes and acronyms, the audience just stood there and looked. Following that event, he decided to listen more to the feedback from Marshall. Moreover, Artis worked to adapt his speeches to the cultures of his many audiences.

Marshall believes the key to their enjoyable career is having fun together. Kirby is not a men's club. Anyone can rise to success in this company. Artis delivered that message by his example and inspirational speaking, of which continues to this day. In many cases, Kirby is the best opportunity for people to create success *without barriers*. Artis and Marshall's friendship has continued to this day. *Together* they made more of a difference than anyone thought they could. Artis always delivers a spectacular job! People just love him! People feel this way largely because he believes, "You have to go down to the people level and bring them up." Thus, one has to understand different perspectives. Regardless of the differences, try to relate, empathize, discern where others are coming from and sincerely try to help. Marshall now works for Preferred Credit, in charge of Kirby parts. He wanted to provide these encouraging words to Artis:

> *When all is said and done, athletes end up with something they can be proud of, such as a legacy, people you met along the way, individuals you've touched, and trusting relationships developed. Enjoy your life, help your kids get what they want out of Kirby, work at leaving a legacy, continue to be a leader and mentor to those people. Most of all, thank you for contributing these values to my life and so many others around the world.*

The Kirby Psychology of Managing Different Personalities

Diagnosis vs. Prognosis

Remember, the mind is like a parachute. It is no good unless it is open. Therefore, diagnose the situation at hand so you can develop the right prognosis. Leading various personalities is a developed skill and determined will. There are not 100 percent workable solutions. The key is understanding the variables of diversity to maximize your goals. The key to leading diverse personalities is your approach, skill set, experience, discernment, and knowledge of individuals.

A Major Key

Diagnose things objectively instead of applying them personally. This will ensure your prognosis maintains an objective overtone. For example, doctors practice medicine and prescribe treatment. The key is engagement of "practice, drills, and rehearse" to ensure the development never becomes personal. There is always room for improvement! In time, you will feel better about the diversity, challenges, and your workforce. Therefore, consider these important attributes when leading development of various personalities:

1.   Diversity
2.   Circumstances
3.   Intent
4.   Objectivity
5.   Management philosophy
6.   Your goal

Diversity

Diversity means inclusion of differences and accepting these differences as a part of growth understanding and development. Thus, considering the diversity of a person is key to understanding skill in leading personalities. One has to consider the culture, ethnicity, gender, ideology, as well as the person's overall objective. Your progress will always have a greater retention and the results with greater success.

Circumstances

Our circumstances are results of our past. However, it is not our future, only our present situation. We lead personalities and develop by considering the circumstances of the person. When you do this, you have a greater insight and vision in determining a workable solution. You gather insight of the individual to see if their adjustment can fit the company's goals. Next, your prognosis can be cost-effective, before investing too much time and resources.

Intent

This refers to our motives and objectives. Be sure to lead personalities by including the intent of the person. When you do this, you take note of their motives and a greater understanding of the person. You cannot read their minds and hearts. However, you can draw conclusions from their behavior and discern their motivation. You will make progress for a greater progression toward success.

Objectivity

Always operate from objectivity instead of a personality point of view. Consider the objectives of a person. By considering their goals, you are able to help them overcome their challenges. You neutralize misunderstandings and hardships. Because you view things differently, you will then explore ways to make things work for the good of everyone involved. Then, you will not allow the different types of personalities to override your objectives. You see the good in the situation and strive to meet the person where the hurt is or the overall concern. Thus, your progress moves beyond current your circumstances.

Management Philosophy

Scrutinize your business by STOPPING doing what you know does not work. Do more of what you know works! Become creative, innovative, and open to taking risks, or attempt new things. Learn how these work.

- Recruit every week. New people are the life-sustaining function of the business. Such recruits will keep you grounded in the business.
- Facilitate daily sales and management meetings thirty minutes earlier each day.
- Lead Saturday meetings thirty minutes early by showing up fifteen minutes in advance.
- Call distributor trainees every morning to gain the metric of yesterday's activity and sales count, and give them a message as a thought for their meetings for the day.
- Consider investing in a customer relationship management (CRM) technology systems to capture sales data in the field via cell phones and in real time.
- Do more of what does work on a consistent and established pattern.
- Be creative, innovative, and attempt new approaches to experience growth personally, emotionally, mentally, and economically.

In life, we have regrets or fulfillments. We can identify patterns in our thinking and language. Patterns can affect our thinking proactively versus reactively. When communicating (and thinking), consider replacing the following words with language to ignite positive following through and plans of action! For example, replace the following words:

Word Choices: Override the negatives with positives

Negative Thinking Patterns (Reactive)	Positive Thinking and Language (Proactive)
I can't!	Instead, say, "I CAN!"
I hope . . .	Instead, say, "I KNOW . . ."
If . . .	Instead, say, "WHEN . . ."
I'll try!	Instead, say, "I WILL!"
But . . .	Instead, say, "AND . . ."

Use these words to start and finish your statement or sentence. Such words will help you become more proactive instead of reactive. Your brain and mind will lean more toward reaching the goals instead of becoming stagnated toward the result.

YOUR GOAL

A GOAL NOT SET IS A GOAL NOT MET. A GOAL NOT MET IS A GOAL NOT SET! You will never reach the fulfillment of a goal without planned action toward the finish. Knowledge is pursued, I believe, to contribute to a better world and fulfilling life. It is about YOU, people attempting to understand what makes their business tick. To make it better, you think logically and consistently about the challenges (problems) when you are able to determine (cause and effect) the relationships between your actions and results. As mentioned, always remember there is a GOLD MINE, in your GOAL MIND. Therefore, define and refine your goals.

Retaining People and Profits

The key to success is HOW you handle a little bit of money before you start making more money.

—*Herb*

Within in the African American community, sometimes money management is our challenge. We get money, wear it, spend it, party with it, and we do not KEEP it!

Herb, Distributor Trainer

The Kirby business can deliver a great amount of money fast! When you develop skill and experience, you have no doubt about your ability. Thus, you know to deliver, and as mentioned, you can generate money fast. Kirby's sales dealers know they can generate fast money based on their ability. Thus, it is hard for new dealers to break away and pursue other careers. Because after they learn and know the basics, they also never forget how profitable they can become in a short amount of time. You will realize your entire success or failure is contingent upon your attitude and commitment to the task.

The money management challenge starts in how you handle a little bit of money. For example, the habit of receiving a wealth of money and blowing it is similar to a phenomenon exhibited by undisciplined athletes. Therefore, with this process, I learned that when my cash flow was low, I needed to become strategic with what I spent. In addition, it was important to understand how much is required to accomplish business goals and live. I became very efficient and strategic in managing incoming money and outgoing money spent. Therefore, by the time I became a distributor trainee, I was almost terrified to spend money wastefully. Mr. Webb would call me and ask, "Herb, have you picked up the money from the finance company you earned this week?" I responded, "Yes!" He would often confirm and ask, "Is the money in the bank? Are you going to invest in Kirbys and merchandise?" Herb thought, "Yes, it can be spent. I don't have to wait a whole week to spend it." Herb was on such a regiment of managing a small amount of money until he became an expert on managing small crises. In addition, his discipline provided the Head Rhino mind-set required to endure rainy days ahead. Knowing and understanding it may not always be pleasant all the time.

> *Small-business owners struggle to master this talent.*
> *In Kirby, you learn this first.*
>
> *—Herb*

Small businesses invest a huge amount of money to gain mastery over mastering money management. However, in Kirby, this is the first thing you learn, because the first thing you recognize is that "you don't have any money!" Therefore, it is critical that you first master your incoming cash flow or money management competency. First, realize you will always have obligations. Will you be able to pay them or not? You may lose stuff or sacrifice things and get it back. Nevertheless, focus on what you CAN DO, not on what you cannot do, understanding you cannot change the element. There are some things you cannot fix. So do not worry about them until you can fix them. Thus, it simplifies your ability to function more progressively.

Webb's philosophy is based on an old Bible testament that encourages us to tithe 10 percent of our earnings. However, Webb believes you have to pay yourself first. He views himself as an obligation—a power bill, a house payment, a car note, etc., those things that are a necessity for the basics and quality of life. You do not want those obligations turned off.

This sales leaders view themselves as a no. 1 priority in the same category. By placing themselves as the priority, they will always have lights and other obligations function at an optimal level. Most people see their greatest necessities as greater than they do, and when they start taking care of themselves, they do not feel good about themselves or have a balanced view of themselves and their work. If you do not have money, then you have to make it a point to have a great work ethic in everything you do.

For example, what if I had to select from two options: (a) Would I pay the rent, or buy Kirbys first? (b) Would I pay the house payment, or buy Kirbys first? Yes, I would buy Kirbys first. The business will keep everything else going. The people have to see me first as a successful businessperson. I am responsible for people's lives. They cannot see me going out of business. If this becomes the case, they will lose confidence to invest in this business. If I am promoting an opportunity or positive attitude, I have to execute this vision. They can never see any blemishes in me or the business. IF they do, it affects their value, investment, and management of the business.

If you made $100 and you have to pay expenses out of that, pretend you only made $90 then pay the expenses. You'll always be taken care of if you pay or manage yourself first. Then pay out or manage other things second. People try to manage themselves first but lack the business aptitude. Most people do not have this level of critical thinking, which causes them to lose focus, confidence, desire, and drive to keep working.

For example, if you have $5,000 and believe in the business, you will put your money in inventory first, because you are good enough to deliver! However, what if you took $5,000 and purchased a car, paid a bill, and believed your credit is good? Now you cannot buy merchandise. If you do not believe in the business, you are raping the business. However, if you take the same amount, invest in the business, then you are forced to use your SKILL and WILL to be productive. Now you can triple $5,000 to $15,000 or $20,000 whereas before that dollar for dollar, $5,000 is $5,000 and that is it! Therefore, instead of worrying about what you cannot control, just stay focused on selling and controlling what you can.

Most people go out to buy a car, take care of STUFF, and defer investment to someone else, instead of investing in him or her to become successful. The first investment should be in you. Why should you feel good about you when you have to go to work and do not have money for gas or other necessities? It is a different mind-set. However, when you pay yourself first, then you are PAID first (Clason's *The Richest Man in Babylon*) before you deposit the money. Write a check for yourself and invest 10 percent to save for your next opportunity.

Small-business owners invest a huge amount of time and money to gain mastery over their money management strategies. However, in Kirby, this is the first challenge. In the beginning, you may not start with a huge amount of money. Thus, it is critical for you to first master this money management competence. Added to this, realize you will always have bills, overhead, and obligations. You will be able to pay for these or not. The outcome depends upon how you structure your overhead and budget. Sometimes you may lose stuff and get it back. Therefore, focus on what you CAN DO instead of what you cannot do. Understand you cannot change the *e*lements. However, you can *r*espond to the challenge or situation. This approach will help you control the outcome. Sometimes you can fix it, and other times you may not. Most important, do not worry about it until you can fix it. This will keep you focused on priorities. Thus, it simplifies your ability to focus and function properly.

Retaining People: ONE-ON-ONE COACHING

You become great based on how you get up from failure, not based on how you are at the top.

—*Artis Webb*

It is so important for management and leadership to take sales teams aside and tell them explicitly what they need to do to achieve success! Place them on a definite program. Otherwise, when they attend sales meetings, some believe every message is for them. Management can provide observations. However, one-on-ones are opportunities to focus on getting the training alignment right. If you do not tell somebody what he or she should focus on, the person will think everything is about them. Therefore, listen attentively and empathetically.

Individual training retained me in the business.

—*Herb*

The greatest learning experiences that Herb gained from Mr. Webb were his interpersonal skills and authentic focus on people. This evolution is similar to "selling Kirbys turned on or turned off and being a man who always saw the good in people." Herb realized he was not a manager or a leader, but a glorified dealer. People benefit from explicit directions. Seeing the consistency of how Webb developed people, especially when they started with less skill than normal, proved inspiring. Herb agreed, "If I could be half as good in that department, I could become a multimillionaire in developing people." Because it does not matter what is going on; it is all about the growth of people. They make the money as well as become the boss or entrepreneur. An individual may arrive with low self-esteem, low work ethic, and some are content with minimum wage earnings and believe making ten dollars an hour equates to the ultimate success in life. However, these same individuals can evolve into *attitudes of excitement* when they develop, go out, and create their own opportunities by following a tried and proven program.

Team Management

Mr. Webb's teams always maintain salespersons at different levels. The team is made up of people of different calibers (cultures and diversity backgrounds). Nevertheless, Mr. Webb teaches and considers every person no matter what his or her level of competence. Therefore, instead of just driving salesperson to appointments, an important role is for the team leaders to develop people with the goal of becoming self-sufficient. Everyone wants a team leader or manager who accomplished his or her *Five-Diamond Medallion statuses* or accomplished *five qualifying months*. Mr. Webb enjoys teaching team leaders, managers, and distributor trainees the program. This training structure can help them realize their full potential. Some traveled and worked with Mr. Webb in the field together as teams for several months. These dealers became self-sufficient. Mr. Webb believes you can become a multimillionaire in business and make money, but you have to become very skilled in dealing with people. Greatness arrives based on how you get up from failure, not how you get to the top. More than any other business, you can rebound here. People aspire to follow your example and formula for success.

Mr. David Kayne, Former Divisional Supervisor and Mentor

David Kayne arrived at Kirby after serving as a military pilot for four and a half years. In 1986, Kirby allowed him to achieve his dream of entrepreneurship. David's career in Kirby evolved from serving as a dealer, distributor trainee, distributor, and divisional supervisor for over twenty years. David enjoyed his run with Kirby. When he initially arrived, he was completely broke with $30,000 in the hole. Today, he enjoys retirement as a double-digit millionaire. His family is comfortable, and he enjoys nurturing the talents of his seventeen-year-old son, a pilot following the path of his father.

In fact, in 1988, David noticed Artis's outstanding qualities of leadership, teamwork, and discipline. David met Artis while he served as national sales manager. David was a distributor. During one disappointing experience in California, Artis reached out to Kayne to explore if they could meet for dinner. This meeting forged the beginnings of an authentic relationship—mentor to mentor.

The relationship evolved beyond that point. Both Artis and David were strongheaded and strong-spirited visionaries. Nevertheless, both remained on the same page and best of friends. Because these leaders respected each other's opinion, they combined their synergies to develop opportunities. Artis eventually became Dave Kayne's supervisor. During this time, David was president of the divisional committee (the committee picks out five distributors). Thus, both shared memorable moments together. In time, Kayne became Artis's supervisor for three years. This team worked very closely together. Kayne shares, "Artis was my best supporter when he was a supervisor!"

What made Artis stand out was his value as a team player. He knew his supervisor and supported his successful endeavors. Thus, Artis is someone that everyone respected, a positive influencer! Artis experienced some of his best years when Kayne served as a divisional supervisor. The future for Artis is to remember people are looking up to him. Thus, I am confident he will continue to "pay it forward," uphold his responsibility as mentor and leader, and teach the next generation to do so. *"Thank you, Artis!"—David Kayne*

Although he will support your success, he expects you to give back. He will hold you to that!

—Artis Webb

Artis shared his admiration for David Kayne. When David assumed the role as divisional supervisor, his vision and diversity enriched people of different cultures. Further, Artis enjoyed the way David worked from the standpoint of helping people to become multimillionaires and entrepreneurs. Some of David's most unforgettable questions include, Would you pay you the money you are expecting to make? What would be your job responsibility? Would you hold yourself accountable to make sure you do that? In addition, he takes a personal interest in another person's success. This made David an outstanding businessperson and giver! Although he will support your success, he expects you to give back. He will hold you to that! He is an unforgettable mentor and friend. —Artis Webb

Will vs. Skill

- Your degree of skill will take you to a level of competency, because you are trained, taught, and you can implement this knowledge. This strategy increases your will to succeed.
- Your will takes you further to abstract levels beyond your consciousness. Will helps you develop the vision, mind-set, and belief that your success is assured.

Challenge your will to go beyond your skill sets. A doctor can operate on a person and say, "This is all I can do!" A person's *will to live* will give them a greater desire for health improvement than drugs. One of my favorite quotes is, "A person convinced against their will is of the same mind still [or opinion still]." This mind-set inspires focus and strict discipline. Sometimes, Herb would do things in his presentation far ahead of his trainee's comprehension because of his vision and follow through of techniques learned in training class. Another critical competency for managers and team leaders is the ability to build and manage effective relationships.

BE a role model.

—A. J. Webb

As a leader, AJ works hard to nurture an inclusive team environment. This delivery arrives by making sure every salesperson, regardless of sale competence, is at ease. This empowers them to transfer varied levels of people skills to their customers. He is very congenial with customers and great at building relationships. Some customers refer to him as their son. AJ believes his positive attitude and organization is important for new salespersons, because your team will notice it IF you are not focused or organized. Looking out for the team, AJ tries to make sure to maintain his superior level of focus and image as a role model. In addition, he is very humble by picking like-minded folks who are humble and approachable. One of AJ's key in gaining commitment from people is setting an example that would inspire the teams' trust and value of themselves. AJ has proven this outstanding approach of developing people. Artis taught him to approach salespersons and treat the team members like customers. For example, when you work with a customer, you will put up with whatever you need to endure in an attempt to gain their business or respect. However, sometimes we are not willing to do the same to develop our team or sales force. However, this salesperson could become a repeat dealer ten or fifteen times a month. Therefore, why not have the same approach to find ways to connect, build rapport, and then increase the credibility and value of what you have to offer to the customer? This focus will instill the right attitude required to help team members embrace their goals. A new salesperson's level of confidence is the level of confidence they have in you—the team leader. These are new people working on blind faith. Therefore, they will receive their fuel and energy from your confidence. Therefore, if you work hard to set the RIGHT example and inspire the BEST performance, everything else will work out; confident dealers *will develop*. Another important quality of a role model is to look like a professional. This visual can help nurture confidence in your credibility as a salesperson.

The Impact of a Professional Image

> *During the first ten to fifteen minutes in the house, you won't*
> *be able to sell a Kirby, but within those first fifteen*
> *to twenty minutes, you could blow the sell.*

> —A. J. Webb

Organization is a competency AJ picked up over the years. He or she is not naturally organized, but can develop this as a habit through trial and error. The structure facilitates delivery to the customers. Professionalism is another trait AJ requires of his team. Normally, people will not give you a chance if you do not convey your first impression. During the first ten to fifteen minutes in the house, you will not be able to sell a Kirby. However, within the first fifteen to twenty minutes, you could blow the sell, because people and customers develop split-second impressions (good or bad) about you. Thus, look at yourself and ask, Would I let myself in this house? Would I let someone that I did not know that looked like me in his or her home? Would I buy products of merchandise from someone who looked and dressed like me? Therefore, the first impression is very important and critical in conveying an enduring professional message. Most people will not give you another chance if you lack the first impression. This opens doors and builds rapport before you start your selling presentation. Make a friend by helping them relax in their own home. Relate to your customers by sharing things you have in common. Such steps will help develop a relationship before the sales process.

Twenty Reasons to Build a Pipeline and Recruit Talent

- New recruits represent the LIFE BLOOD of the business.
- It's the only CONTROL you have in the business.
- It's the first sign of GROWTH in the business.

- It creates a STRUCTURE for your business.
- It sets a PATTERN AND IMAGE for your business.
- This establishes an "INFRASTRUCTURE" and office location for your business.
- It facilitates, DELEGATES, and creates personal responsibility as well as opportunity for others in your business (office assistant, service, and consumerism).

- It SHARPENS your managerial and leadership skills in the business.
- It is the PREREQUISITE for the formation of relationships required for a successful business.

- It provides VALIDITY to your business.
- It establishes the DEPARTMENTS needed for GROWTH for the BUSINESS (administration, sales, service, accounting, etc.).

- It establishes OFFICE HOURS, WORK ETHICS, and PROFESSIONALISM, and CONSISTENCY in the BUSINESS.

- It isolates your MAIN OBJECTIVES, defines your PHILOSOPHY, and implements your PROGRAMS in the BUSINESS.

- It assists in reaching your GOALS and allows you to DEVELOP and REPLACE STAGNATION and MEDIOCRITY through new people for the continuous GROWTH of the BUSINESS.

- It reminds you of your INTENT to RECRUIT, TRAIN, MOTIVATE, RETAIN, and PROMOTE people through the BUSINESS (one-third coming into the business, one-third growing via upward movement, one-third departing for other opportunities, most importantly, respecting the attrition of BUSINESS).

- It measures your personal GOALS, GROWTH, FINANCIAL INCREASE, and DEVELOPMENT in the BUSINESS.

- It allows you to PROMOTE people in a timely manner and move to the next level of the business.

- It gives you an opportunity to DELEGATE and see your growth philosophy through others you brought through the business.

- It keeps you in GOOD STANDING with your distributors, supervisor, and company, thus permits you to break away in the business.

- IT'S THE RIGHT THING TO DO. IT'S THE ONLY WAY YOU WILL GROW your business long term. You can relive your success vicariously through others in the business.

- Now, from these series of fundamentals, if or when you do all these suggestions, how many sales do you think will come your way?

- You will personify your success to a level of hundred plus, Golden Circles, and ultimately become a platinum distributor. You will definitely grow to your maximum capacity.

Webb-Based Reflective Effective Audit

IF YOU died tonight, would your practice of grooming emerging leaders build a foundation of success for growth, innovation, and development of people? Does your team consider you a role model? What type of image does your team project to specific communities? As an individual, what can you do to project a more professional image? As a manager and leader, what can you do to leave the team stronger than found? Jot down your responses and goals below.

1.

2.

3.

CHAPTER 7

Sales Strategy #4:
Get with the Program

*The Unstoppable Charging
Rhinocust!*

A program is a preset, pretested set of guidelines that have already proven successful. It will work automatically every time. If you could digest that thought, we will not ask you to do anything unproven to create success. One of the best ways to stick to the program is to charge like a rhinocust. Nothing stops a rhinocust! A rhino charges, but the rhinocust is unstoppable. Combine rhino and locust = rhinocust, and they keep on charging! Determine in your mind that you are a RHINOCUST. Even if a fire were blazing through the jungle, the locust body would exhibit certain types of chemical enzymes that seem to generate more locusts. The rhinocusts could continue charging through, until it appears they are unstoppable. The rhinocust knows that with every obstacle, there is a solution. The greatest mistake is giving up. Nothing in the world can take away or take the place of persistence. This quality can overcome resistance. You cannot be financially successful until you share your success with others. Therefore, I recognized my responsibility is to share my success. In today's economy, it is critical to have strong believers and closers. The rhinocust attitude can keep you moving forward through obstacles. Here is the rhinocust formula to help you through critical challenges and to keep you moving forward: rhino + locusts = unstoppable! Therefore, adopt the philosophy of a rhinocust and become indomitable! You have the invaluable strength to do whatever it takes to succeed.

Closing Sales: The Ten Steps for Rhinocusts to Charge Forward

1. **See how far we can PUSH.**
   - Persevere until something happens, persevere until sales happen, persevere until success happens.
2. **Find a true objection.**
   - People may give excuses, but find the true objections. This is why you want to go through the top ten reasons people say no.
3. **Isolate the objection.**
   - Inquire if this is the only reason they are not buying. Objections indicate interest. Find a palatable way to overcome it.
4. **Learn from the experience.**
   - You need to know the next time you encounter a similar situation how to navigate the customer to next level.
5. **Recognize the pattern.**
   - People may say yes or no; it does not matter. As long as you recognize the pattern, you'll have the conviction to keep pushing forward.
6. **See if they are sincere.**
   - We only want to sell if they are sincerely interested. We don't' want to sell to people who do not like it, want it, or need it. We will be friends if they buy, friends if they do not buy. We are there to first establish trust and customer service.
7. **See if we have exhausted every means.**
   - Know this in your heart so you can gain the fortitude for the next presentation.
8. **Develop the mental toughness.**
   - During these economic woes, we especially need to have mental toughness. We are a rhinocust—we are charging and are unstoppable!
9. **Know what it takes to be no. 1.**
   - It is critical to determine what it takes to get the best out of yourself, to work a full day in order to continue on without letup.
10. **Understand why we missed the sale or made it.**
    - It does not matter about the outcome as long as we understand why and learn from the experience. Make it a learning curve.

IF your *WHY* does not make you cry, you are not pushing hard enough or are emotionally connected to it. Never use any type of negative energy to bring about a positive outcome. This mind-set will circumvent your long-term logics for success. Nevertheless, "the teacher will arrive when the student is ready to learn" (Buddha). Therefore, focus on becoming better rather than bitter. Make failure your teacher and not your undertaker.

Webb-Based Science Reflective Effective Audit

What parts of the program seem easier? Alternatively, what parts of the program present a challenge? How can you become an unstoppable rhinocust sales leader? Jot down some goals you plan to execute today to stick to the program.

1.

2.

3.

CHAPTER 8

Sales Strategy #5:
Know the Sales Formula for Success

*Simply maintain a positive attitude, stick with your
program and follow-through."*

—Artis Webb

The Sales Success Formula

Variable Symbol	Definition	The Look
E	Events	Rain, snow, elements, zero appointments, etc.
R	Response	You can reject or respond. Project the right or wrong attitude.
O	Outcome	Frustration, anxiety, depression, or success. A positive attitude, sticking with the program produces a logical and balanced point of view.

Events (E)

Events are things we experience and maintain no control over in life. These may include the weather, other people, attitude, behaviors, etc. For example, a distributor might complain, "I've had this distributorship for six months. The trouble is, I bust my butt every day, and can't get this business going for the last six months!" *Instead of discouragement over this event,* simply maintain a positive attitude—stick with your program and follow-through. Accept events at face value.

Response (R)

Above is the *distributor's response* to his situation or event. Instead of focusing on what he can do, the results are frustration, anxiety, or depression. This is an example of a response to events. Therefore, focus on responding to the task instead of reacting to things you have no control over. Allow your reasonableness to take control versus your emotions. Maintain a balanced point of view. Logic opens the mind, and emotions close the ear.

Outcome (O)

Outcome is a result of what shows up because of E + R. *People always complain about outcomes* and blame events. "We're out of inventory?" Someone arrives late and complains about traffic when they know how important it is to leave home early. If someone was unsuccessful in scheduling appointments or securing a presentation, they blame the weather. You cannot control events, you cannot control the weather, you cannot control the economy, and you cannot control the customer, but you can control your attitude response. This is your response. If you do not like the outcome, you have to change the way you respond. That is the assurance of the formula. That is your point of power!

Your Point of Power IS Your Response

The formula is the only way to change the outcome. For example, in mathematics: $2 + 2 = 4$. If you want 5 you need to go back to change the response in the formula, not the event. All you can control is your reaction and response, your point of power. When you accept this formula and control your response, you are bound to increase positive outcomes. If you want the answer to become 5, then the event, which represents 2, remains the same. The response must change from 2 to 3 to arrive to an outcome of 5.

LOR—Law of Reciprocity

The law of reciprocity says that whatever you put into something, that is exactly what you will get out of it. Reciprocity is like the law of gravity—you always get the same results regardless. It does not discriminate, male or female, small or large. It is a law set in stone with absolute accuracy. Always the same results, because gravity falls thirty-two feet per second. It is like the biblical law in Galatians 5:22, 23, "You will reap what you sow." Whatever you put into it, you will get out. Regardless of the plant you reap, the outcome can only produce according to its kind. It is not contingent upon your attitude. Therefore, consider these examples. When you go to work, always strive to do these minimums:

- Three presentations or sales calls per day
- Three personal recruits per day
- Three solid appointments per day
- Three sales deliveries per week
- Make a plan to work your plan

You WILL deliver successful results and become destined to succeed at your goals _IF_

> you want to reach a goal bad enough to go out and fight for it! To work day and night for it. To make sacrifices for it. To work long hours for it and work weekends for it. IF all you dreamed and schemed is about was it, and life seems worthless and useless without it, if you simply go after the goal with all your capacity, sagacity, faith, hope, and stern per tenacity. If neither cold, poverty, famine, sickness, pain of body, brain and gout can keep you away from the goals you want. If dogged and grimed you beseeched it, you will beset it. With the help of God, you will get it. Give out, but do not give up. Because you will succeed! If you gladly sweat for it, fret for it, and lose all your terror and opposition for it. You will succeed because there is no excuse. (Les Brown)

Webb-Based Reflective Effective Audit

Mr. Webb is inspired by Les Brown's drive to do whatever required in reaching and achieving his goals. Reflect on ways you have responded to events in the past. Based on Mr. Webb's insight, what are some new ways you can respond to increase successful outcomes? Write down three scenarios. Share these with your team. Include ways you will respond more proactively to events to increase successful outcomes.

1.

2.

3.

Chapter 9

Sales Strategy #6:
Become Customer Centric

I've learned that people will forget what you said, people will forget what you did, but people will never forget how you made them feel.

—*Maya Angelou*

Sales are a people business built on relationships. Therefore, always engage and give value to the client from beginning to end. One way we are able to satisfy our customer is by gaining the prospect's trust and reaction before departure. Whether the prospect decides to purchase or not, we will treat all with dignity and respect. In addition, we value their input by taking a few moments to ask their opinion. Follow these steps for customer-centric success.

1. What impressed you about the Kirby or product (isolate three things)?
2. Always thank them, demonstrate appreciation for the customer's time, inquire in comparison with their product, and explore why they mentioned certain things they like better about your product.

3. Expound upon the three-year limited warranty, lifetime rebuilding warranty, and fire protection plan. Compare this value with other products on the market.

4. Inquire, if they had your product in their home, where would be the first place they would use it?

5. Would you recommend the product to family and friends? If so, write them a referral sheet.

6. Do they see a need for the product in their home today? When would they like to start using the product (since they see a need for it)?

7. Explore the best plan for customers: budget or cash plan.

8. Assume the sale by reaching out your hand and welcoming them to the Kirby family. Outline their payment plan of choice.

9. Allow the customer to decide. If they have a need for the Kirby, ask what circumstances prevent them from purchasing and have the customer sign the customer reaction sheet to confirm completion of the presentation. Take to heart their suggestions, provide documentation and consummation of the sales, as well as follow through with other referrals or appointments received.

Webb-Based Science Reflective Effective Audit

How can you do a better job at building rapport and relationships with customers? What are some authentic ways to keep them engaged during every step of the way? Jot down what you learned from your last appointment and, in addition, new approaches you will apply today.

1.

2.

3.

CHAPTER 10

Sales Strategy #7:
Close with Excellence and Skill

The Head Rhino Challenge

Ten reasons why you should close after a customer says no. We do this to

1. see how far we can push for the close,
2. find the true objection,
3. isolate it as the only reason,
4. learn from the experience,
5. recognize the pattern the next time,
6. see if the customer is sincere,
7. explore if you have exhausted every means,
8. develop mental toughness,
9. know what it takes,
10. understand why we either sold or missed the opportunity.

Top Ten Closing Reasons Explained

1. To see how far we can PUSH (persevere until something happens). How?
   a. Ask questions. Did you like it, see a need for it, or why would you prefer our product to yours?
   b. Confirm your answers. Thank you. We appreciate your sincere honesty.
   c. Listen to the response. Listen and feel their response empathetically.

2. To find the true objection. You do that by doing the following:
   a. Eliminating excuses, such as a spouse, affordability, not being in the market, a priority, and the price.

    b.   Listening for consistency. Note their tone, countenance, and body language.

    c.   Narrowing it down. This skill will allow you to hear of loss or perceive their response.

3. To isolate it as the only reason they will not buy. You do this by doing the following:

    a.   Ask the customer what the main reason for their position is.

    b.   Focus on their timing and desire to own.

    c.   Now is this the only reason? Draw out their main objection.

    d.   If it wasn't for _____, would you ___ or when would you consider? Accept their yes or no equally with the same enthusiasm.

4. To learn from the experience. You do this by doing the following:

    a.   Repeating or restating the questions. Reference a third party. For example, do you see why people buy this product?

    b.   Reinforce and emphasize the benefits. Ask them to express the features and if they would benefit from these features.

    c.   Express and give examples why people buy. Share personal stories and examples of how you have personally benefitted from the product as well as others.

5. To recognize the pattern for the next time. How?

    a.   Remember, sales made leave clues. Express your observation of their like, want, and need from your perspective.

    b.   Missed sales leave clues. Express why they continue to keep purchasing other products to take care of the same problem and getting the same results. These lines of reasoning help you discern the next steps.

    c.   Read their expression properly to allow them to feel this is already their decision instead of yours.

6. To see if they are really sincere.

    a.   Observe their response. As you ask questions, discern through their humor and the sincerity of their expressions.

    b.   Observe their interest. Discern why they feel the way they do about your product.

    c.   Observe their behavior. See if they are eager to use it, touch it, feel it, or participate in the operation.

7. To see if we exhaust every means. How?

    a.   Promote contests—creates a now factor or reason to buy.

    b.   Promote other specials—savings and discounts.

    c.   Savings by leaving the demonstration model—prevents your having to maintain a presentation model.

8. To develop mental toughness. How?

    a.   Maintain your optimism. Always promote positive vibes toward the sale.

    a.   Believe they will buy regardless. Never let them see you sweat or show a "give up" attitude.

    b.   Never stop assuming the sale. Be natural by assuming this is common for people to reflect after seeing your product and naturally buy it.

9. To know what it takes. You do this by doing the following:

    a.   Third-party assistance—using all your resources available.

    b.   Qualify for ROL program. Ask for referrals, optional offers, and let them make their decision.

    c.   Ask for the order and welcome them to the Kirby family.

    a.   Invite them to be a part of the millions of satisfied customers around the globe.

10. To understand why we sold or missed the sale. How?

    a.   Express three reasons people work (what they like, want, and need).

    b.   You like it, want it, and deserve it (why not take advantage of the offer?).

    c.   Give you reason you should buy and not buy. Become the customer. Be friendly regardless of the outcome of their decision.

Webb-Based Science Reflective Effective Audit

Artis maintains a 92.3 percent closing average (out of sixty presentations to qualified customers, his outcomes would score 90 percent or higher). Mr. Webb received a six-figure salary as Kirby's national sales manager. The highest bonus he received is $80,000. However, the people he trained superseded him in earnings. Thus, this indicates there is no limit to your opportunity and earnings.

He thought he was cheating life. We cannot defy gravity; however, he defies gravity in Kirby. Thus, regardless of the case or load he's carrying, he knows he has the same opportunity. He has to increase his goals for success before gravity arrives. What is your closing average? Which styles mentioned above could you apply today to improve your closing success?

1.

2.

3.

PART IV

Legacy: What Type of Sales Leader Will You Become?

You can IF you think you can!

—Henry Ford and Mom Webb

George Washington Carver once shared, "When you do the common things in life in an uncommon way, you will command the attention of the world." It is true that occasionally we do not recognize the greatness among us. One way in which I enriched the barometer of greatness. He is cognizant that it was not how much wealth that one acquires, but it was having a vision with standards, integrity, values, convictions, and the ability to affect those around him positively.

As a child, Artis's mother always said, "*You can if you think you can!*" Therefore, your thoughts are the most powerful and greatest influence of your personal growth. When I was young and growing up, my mother used to say, "The road to the top will always be rough. There is no easy way, but if you believe you can do it, there will not be a single person to stop you! Because "YOU CAN if you think you can!" Day in and day out, she would repeat this to me. Each time, she would look straight at me. I never doubted what she said to be true. I just was not sure what I was supposed to do. As a child, we often received point-blank direction. However, I lacked the context required to piece the puzzle together.

Then one day, when I needed her help, the context arrived. Little did I know this was her plan. I overcame her objection by saying, "You can if you think you can!" A smile swept across her face. I even saw a tear and finally repeated her words. She told me not to FEAR (false evidence appearing real) because "*no* doesn't mean never. It really means not yet! Learn to try a (little harder) and you'll get what you want in life!" My mother is no longer by my side. Although we are apart, the philosophy she taught me as a child fuels my determination as an adult. She will always be with me, within her heart! Believing has power! Even scientists are unable to figure it out! As you build your career as a sales leader, never forget about those that came before you. Because you can if you think you can and become what you think about most.

Dedicated to Dave Stewart

If it were not for Dave Stewart's ability to lead, train, and inspire me, I might still be working for $2.69 an hour, struggling from paycheck to paycheck. This role model and father figure taught and gave me the foundation to build a successful career in the Kirby business. He always taught me the power of positive thinking. This hero groomed me as the Head Rhino.

In Kirby we teach the wisdom of sales—the priority.

—Dave Stewart

In America, success reflects large homes, expensive cars, and nice clothes. If permitted, the size of one's paycheck can go to our heads and exhibit itself in sizeable egos. Therefore, it might surprise you to meet a millionaire who lives in a modest home, and at ninety years of age, he continues working six days a week. He works just because he loves people. Well, if you have never seen a model, you have not met Mr. Dave Stewart. When he departed from his former career to sell Kirby vacuum cleaners, people thought he was CRAZY.

People thought I was crazy to quit my job to sell vacuum cleaners! However, after I deposited $13,000 in my bank account during my first month, I suddenly became intelligent.

—Dave Stewart

Mr. Stewart arrived to Kirby in September 1952. He trained thousands and has remained in the sales business for over sixty years. His attitude and leadership led him to deliver speeches and educate sales teams at hundreds of locations all over the world. When you consider the purpose of education (Martin Luther King, 1947), the journey should walk us down a road of life exploration, resulting in the realization of a profound need to become more aware, humble, and resourceful. However, sometimes you will meet people with a wealth of education to the exclusion of humility and courage required to go out and simply sell Kirbys or any product. Prior to Mr. Stewart's arrival at

Kirby, he sold shoes and jewelry. He always maintained the utmost respect for women, treating them like queens. When he quit those jobs to sell a vacuum cleaner, people thought he was crazy! Although starting with $600, Stewart became profitable quickly, depositing $13,000 in his bank during the first month. At about this time, the former crowd who perceived him as crazy changed his status to "intelligent." As mentioned, he continues working because serving people makes him feel happy. Yes, Mr. Stewart remains a very humble man worth millions of dollars. Despite decades of success in the business, he confirmed, "If I could go back two years prior, I would still know exactly what to do to create a successful business. I've done it for years . . . and would duplicate success again."

Mr. Stewart believes Kirby sales teams really have to gain a well-rounded understanding of what the program has to offer. People often misjudge the opportunity, believing "They are not going to knock on a door and talk to strangers!"

Therefore, Mr. Stewart always invited new dealers to keep an open mind and "Inspect what you expect." If you are expected to do something, find out what you need to do to accomplish your task. If you do not like the program, then no one is forcing you to work. However, those who choose to stay are assured success, and consequently, he promoted many people. The greatest quality required is "to love what you do!" You have to learn how to have fun! Within his lifetime, Stewart sold Kirbys to political figures, city leadership, and anyone living within a sellable house; he would knock on the door. He always encouraged, "Do not worry about things you have absolutely control over. Concentrate constantly on things you can change."

Then I met Mr. Fantastic!

—Dave Stewart

As mentioned, Artis was the first African American to rise to an executive level in the Kirby Company. Artis stood out because of his desire and drive to succeed. Artis was determined to achieve success even without reliable transportation (because his car was about to be repossessed). He stayed focused and exceeded expectations as a part-time sales dealer and delivered sixteen sales units during his first month. However, sales were not the only areas in which he exhibited discipline. Artis is morally clean, exercises on a daily basis, and is not a man of excesses, and more than anything else, he is a family man. Equipped with his million-dollar smile and interpersonal skills, Artis, or Mr. Fantastic, could not lose. Another important factor for success in Kirby is to have a partner in love and family. Mrs. Webb is a beautiful and extremely intelligent woman. She too excelled in sales. They ran the business and remained wonderful parents.

When you're a new sales dealer, you're filled with frustrations,
uncertainties, and doubt. . . . However, the trainer's role is to help
one overcome uncertainties.

—*Dave Stewart*

Mr. Stewart made a profound impact on Artis's life. He set a high standard as a leader, excellent trainer, and friend. As a leader, he always taught his sales force, "You can grow as big as you want to grow by helping others grow as big as they want to grow." In the world of sales, targets can easily move individuals to create a culture to focus on self alone. Here is where the world of Kirby sets a higher standard and culture for sales. New sales dealers arrive with FUDS (frustrations, uncertainties, doubts, skepticism). Direct sells is scary. However, Kirby will never leave you in the lurch to figure out success on your own. In fact, it is the trainer's role to help his or her sales team overcome uncertainties. Hence, success in this business is built collectively.

First, we provide intrinsic values. On a daily basis, sales teams receive robust and daily inspirational training. However, instead of team leaders returning to an office to wait for numbers or another meeting, team leaders accompany sales dealers to the field with a mission to help them create success. Stewart always focused on developing talents and training sales dealers to help them achieve success. Sales teams need to understand

1.   product knowledge and present the product effectively to customers;
2.   prospecting or direct sales require door-to-door canvassing;
3.   other ways to market the product, such as scheduling appointments from referrals;
4.   closing the sale is no contest when you give a complete and thorough presentation.

Mr. Stewart confirmed he never pressured anyone into buying. He learned a long time ago that the smartest people are women. If you think you are going to outsmart them, consider whether your mother is dumb. Of course not! If you burn people off, they will run you out of town. If you sell and help them solve problems, they will come back and refer new business. Therefore, he taught Artis these skills. In fact he assured, if he followed his program, within twelve months he would become the leader in their division. Thus, it was no surprise when Artis became the no. 1 sales dealer in Mr. Stewart's distributorship.

Therefore, Artis quickly arrived to the management program. His promotion was not without challenges. For example, he had to endure an obstacle of watching his business burn to the ground. This fire incident resulted in the accumulation of a huge amount of debt. However, Mr. Stewart's CRASH (commitment, regimented, attitude, stickability, and hurry) program enabled him to wipe out the debt completely in a short period of ninety days; he gave Artis the crash program! Second, we provide extrinsic values. Appreciation for hard work is the heart and soul of the Kirby business. In fact, if you want to travel, Kirby will take a sales force places people normally could not afford on their own expense: first-class flights, cruises, and tours around the world. After a person achieved first sales goal, we would take the salesperson and spouse out for an evening meal. To motivate his sales team, Mr. Stewart would provide extrinsic rewards in the form of contests. Some of these gifts include cars, trips, and all types of things to appreciate and motivate people. Rewards were provided to demonstrate to the sales team what THEY COULD EXPECT by building a career in Kirby.

The mediocre teacher tells. The good teacher explains. The superior teacher demonstrates. The great teacher inspires.

—William Arthur Ward

Anyone can dispense instructions, e-mail requirements, or tell you what is required to remain in a chair or position. However, it takes a giant of a friend to walk with you as the "guide on the side" and outline a blueprint to build a successful business and career. That is what Mr. Stewart did for Artis. He took Artis under his wings. One of the greatest examples of advice is Mr. Stewart's distributor code of ethics.

Distributor Code of Ethics

I *will* observe the highest standard of character, honesty, and integrity in dealings with my customers, fellow distributors, and other members of the Kirby profession.

I *will* abide by the golden rule, "Do unto others as you would have them do unto you."

I *will* conduct business in a manner, which will command the respect of the members of my profession and set an example for them to follow.

I *will* pledge myself to maintain friendly, ethical relations with fellow distributors and compete with them on a fair and honorable basis.

I *will* respect the authority vested in me by the Kirby company to act in their behalf in serving the public and will strive at all time to the terms of this agreement.

I *will* concentrate on selling only those parties outlined in my Kirby Distributor Agreement and refuse to sell any Kirby merchandise to unauthorized sources.

I *will* respect my customers and make every attempt to solve any complaints and for better customer relations in my market area.

I *will* price my merchandise fairly and attempt to give my customers quick and efficient service at reasonable prices.

I *will* never encourage a Kirby person from a fellow distributor's company to leave and join my organization; instead, I will praise that distributor in the eyes of the fellow worker.

I *will* never do anything to undermine a fellow distributor; instead, I will lend a helping hand whenever the need arises.

I *will* offer Kirby opportunity to everyone in my organization and will strive to help each individual reach his or her goals.

I *realize* that only by unselfish service and dedication can the Kirby profession have the public confidence that it merits, and I will at all times seek to elevate the standards of the Kirby profession by governing my actions and my business according to the provisions of this code and by inspiring my fellow distributors to do likewise. —*David Stewart*

Management of a successful business requires a wealth of moving parts: bankers, certified accountants, day-to-day operations, talent recruitment, etc. Mrs. Webb embraced the business, just like Mr. Stewart's late wife. While he coached Artis on leadership aspects of the business, his wife coached Mrs. Webb on managing the business. Soon Artis became a distributor. Mr. Stewart helped him pick out a great location, remained impressed with his positive attitude and above-average performance. Thus, he was confident that he would continue to become a seasoned and mature professional in the business. As mentioned, today we can see the results of his creative years. As a national sales manager, Artis traveled to seventy-plus countries, spoke salutations of several languages, and always left a positive image wherever he traveled. His leadership example changed lives.

In your fifties, you can peak, because the work invested reaps full harvest. Where people fail, the Kirby program works. Unlike a wealth of companies, Kirby always provides a first-class product along with a lifetime rebuilding warranty. The company is owned by Warren Buffet and maintains a presence in seventy-plus countries. Success is repeated over generations because the business runs on a highly professional level and remains consumer focused. Often Stewart would ask his sales team, "Who's going to win the Super Bowl?" Then he would reply, "The one with fewer errors, because they have proven themselves, whatever they do, they are the best at it!" Artis is a wonderful example of a person who succeeds in this business. The higher you rise, the more polished you become, and a decrease of errors results.

Why was Stewart a great trainer and friend for Artis? First, he addressed the no. 1 area that defines your potential for success: your attitude. In my family or business, we don't talk negative anywhere. Desire is the basis of all achievement; inspect what you expect. Do not worry about things that you have absolutely no control over. Stewart always promoted the power of positive thinking. He believed potential started in the mind. You have to teach yourself the basis of desire. A wealth of successful sales leaders came from nothing. Thus, sales dealers are coached to concentrate constantly on things they can change.

Stewart encouraged this mantra: "Don't worry about anything; everything is a new adventure because you will meet someone new every day." Added to these, he encouraged positive morale, always taking pictures, running contests, awarding cash prizes, and ensuring the entire team achieved success each week. Kirby even provides internships to help students pay for college. One summer, he engaged over twenty college students who wanted to sell vacuum cleaners. However, he required outside assignments to complete prior to arriving at Kirby. Kirby's summer program provides scholarships and cash every month to offices to help dealers pay for college education. Success for Stewart's sales force sold 176 Kirby sells in one day. People arrived from other countries in Europe to explore why his team was so successful!

This is the best carrot in the world for someone
without opportunities.

—*Dave Stewart*

One secret in life is this: you will not have many opportunities in the world to become successful. Kirby has been around one hundred years. Sale teams have walked through Kirby and arrived to a beautiful way of life, out of poverty, and sustained success for family and retirement. In his older years, Mr. Stewart embraces a huge amount of satisfaction and maintains zero regrets in his career of choice. IF he could live his life over again, he would still choose KIRBY as a sales career. As mentioned, Kirby teaches the wisdom of sales as the priority. This wisdom is exhibited in treating people nice. When you do this, people say good things about your reputation and want to do business with you again. Good service leads to retention. As Stewart loved customers, he brought thousands of people into the business. What other sales business could you find an old man still working six days a week and fully equipped with a sharp mental attitude? Although he lost his parents at a young age and his wife has passed on before him, he has zero complaints about life.

Sometimes business leaders invest a lifetime to generate wealth and while sacrificing their relationships with kids and spouses for an eternity. Yet Mr. Stewart's son and daughter still call him on the phone and say, "I love you, Dad!" His son works for SAAS, voted one of the best companies to work for in 2013. He travels all over the world delivering and facilitating seminars to educate high-level leaders on money. To help him become more polished, Stewart recommended his son spend some time with Artis so he could gain training in the field to sell Kirbys. A number of other blessings include one grandson who graduated from college. In addition, his great-great-grandson Leon Thomas (no. 1 distributor in the world of Kirby) entered the Kirby business and shares the same great reward and satisfaction that results from helping people. In closing, Mr. Stewart comments. "It is nice when you wake up every day with a smile on your face and you look forward to going to work."

Dedicated to Bobby Wisinger, Former Division Supervisor

This kid Artis Webb has gone absolutely mad selling Kirbys!

—*Dave Stewart*

In 1972, Artis and Bobby met in Raleigh, North Carolina. Bobby was a divisional supervisor for Dave Stewart, a distributor in the same city, and Artis was a new dealer. Bobby shared, "He was just a brand-new kid!" However, Bobby was immediately impressed with Artis's drive, enthusiasm, and successful selling of Kirbys—more than the average dealer. Artis achieved successful outcomes because of his extra efforts. From the very beginning, Artis wanted to become a leader in Kirby. Thus, Dave Stewart, Artis's factory distributor, reached out to Bobby to share, "This kid Artis Webb has gone absolutely mad selling Kirbys!" Thereafter, Bobby interviewed Artis and listened to his goals, qualified, and extended Artis a special VIP trip to attend a private meeting at the Regency Hyatt Hotel. After Bobby learned of Artis's goals and accomplishments in Kirby, he gave this announcement at the Regency Hyatt Hotel before three hundred people:

> I've met a young man who has been the most outstanding and motivated kid encountered within a long time in this business. From this point forward, Dave Stewart and I will refer to him as Mr. Fantastic!

Artis and Bobby shared similar backgrounds. Bobby arrived to Kirby with a pregnant wife and was laid off as an electrician apprentice; he had no way to earn a living. So he heard of a friend who sold Kirbys. At that time, his mentors informed him, "We cannot find good leaders to sell vacuum cleaners. People don't want to do it. However, we do have money. So take some English courses." Soon Bobby's distributor was promoted, and he arrived too his own office. Later Bobby approaches Adrian Budlong (his VP) to ask for a program and commitment to move to an executive promotion to supervisor. After six months, Bobby would either move somewhere else or build the best distributorship. Following these events, he received a promotion. Just as Bobby receives a promotion from a distributor, he wanted to give the same opportunity to Artis and pay it forward.

What does Bobby love about Artis? Bobby loves Artis's natural way of caring for people and his willingness to share knowledge and develop talents for success in the business. The problem with Artis is, IF you have a commitment, he talks, talks, and talks . . . and if you have something else to do, it is hard to get away. He is Mr. Fantastic!

Today Bobby continues to maintain a close relationship with Artis for years. They still appreciate each other. However, that is what Kirby is all about. This is not a hardcore business but a high-touch environment designed to develop people and take care of customers. Bobby is honored to mentor, sponsor, and support Artist's successes, thus paying his personal appreciation forward!

Dedicated to Jimmy Iorio, Kirby Supervisor

As a goodwill ambassador and outreach distributor, Artis
traveled all over the world motivating other sales forces.

—*Jimmy Iorio*

As a high school dropout, Jimmy started in Kirby at sixteen years of age. Kirby was an opportunity to develop his own paycheck. Now fifty-five years later, he serves as a divisional supervisor for California and Hawaii. Therefore, it was refreshment for him to help build a California division and achieve over thirteen thousand Kirby sales in one month. Jimmy met Mr. Webb in 1989. During this time, he was a top-notch (top-volume) factory distributor and outreach distributor. Because of an accident, Artis was going through hard times. He was hit by a car and laid up for most of the year. Believing he was on his way out, he feared the company would take his people that he invested so much time in to develop.

Another major challenge for Artis was his belief that the company was prejudiced. However, Jimmy did not say he was right or wrong; he simply asked, "What are you going to do about it?" Artis stormed out, convinced Jimmy was not listening to him. Then he returned the next day with this response, "You're right! It does not matter. The truth is, what am I going to do about it?" Therefore, instead of blaming the company, Artis realized nobody can make you feel bad without your permission. He was allowing other people to control him through their negative emotional behavior. Thus, he invested in positive self-talk to move forward. From that point forward, Jimmy and Artis became permanent friends.

Jimmy was one of the top distributors in the country. Thus, he arrived at Artis's office to coach him on ways to improve his business. During this visit Artis's level of production tripled. Artis was glad he came and welcomed feedback. Upon his return home, Jimmy recommended Artis as an outreach distributor. He believed this role would prove good for the Kirby business. Thus, a year later, Artis received appointment as an outreach distributor or ambassador for the Kirby Company. As an outreach distributor, Artis traveled to practically every state in the United States except Vermont to motivate other sales forces.

The Law of Reciprocity

As loyal colleagues, both Artis and Jimmy lived by the law of reciprocity. During a national sales meeting in California, leadership inquired about whom in California would make a great divisional supervisor. Artis promptly recommended Jimmy. Thereafter, Jimmy was a supervisor. In 1992, Artis became national sales manager for the Kirby Company. Within the next eight years, Artis became the greatest national sales manager for the company in the history of one hundred years. He also influenced more lives and inspired many others to achieve their greatness.

Elite of the Elite, Artis Webb

We're not in the vacuum cleaner business; we're in the people business.

—Jimmy Iorio

Back in 1989, Artis needed someone to wake him up and show him HE IS a special human being. This became evident when he was approved as national sales manager and succeeded in motivating over fifteen thousand people worldwide throughout the global world of the Kirby Company. He is an outstanding inspirer and motivator. During any Kirby meeting, you can see the respect that people have for him—although Jimmy served as a divisional supervisor for nineteen years and became one of the first supervisors to sell over five hundred thousand Kirbys and the only division in the world to accomplish this in nine years. Artis played a big part in this successful outcome. Artis is effective in inspiring people because he "meets people where the hurt or concern is . . . he IS THE MASTER!" I often refer to him as the "Black Abe Lincoln because he had to work through so many setbacks, and Lincoln became one of the greatest presidents the country has ever known. We enjoyed creating fun for our sales force! For example, once Artis dressed up as Don King and I pretended to knock him out. This level of culture is important, because we are not in the vacuum cleaner business; we are in the people business. Artis believes what the late Maya Angelou once shared, "People don't care how much you know until they know how much you care." This is the true secret to becoming a good supervisor—letting people know you care, helping them to become greater than they think they are. During every session, Jimmy opened with jokes, because when people are laughing, they are paying attention. The hardest challenge in this business is retention. However, Jimmy notes, "Artis has mastered it, because people cling to him like honey. Positivity can attract somebody. Artis devotes every day of his life to self-improvement and reads more than most people I know!"

Artis and Jimmy push each other. In the sales business, it is important to have someone pushing you to reach your goals; everyone gets negative. If another gets down, we call the other. We have never had a time when both of us were down at the same time. People often say, "I am hanging in there."

Jimmy wonders, "Hanging in there doing what?" Alternatively, they will say, "I think I am going to make it," then he wonders, "Make what?" Life is beautiful, consider the alternative; it is what you MAKE IT. Don't let the universe dictate how you should perceive and live your life. Artis and Jimmy never acted their ages! They still have fun on a daily basis. Both believe their best days are yet to come! *"Artis, I thank and love you, my brother."—Jimmy Iorio*

Dedicated to Salvatore Sorbera, a Colleague and Member of the Dream Team: Artis, Jimmy, and Sal

Being exposed to Artis for six months is better than what you could gain at an Ivy League school.

—*Sal Sorbera*

When you have a positive team that thinks alike, you can make a huge difference in people's lives. Artis, Jimmy, and Salvatore (Sal) traveled all over the world inspiring and motivating people. Artis is unique in his special care for people; he motivates the motivator, full of knowledge, and he inspired Sal by being positive and sharing motivational words. The outcome led to a change in the way he approached life. This mind-set is important for new salespersons. From the very beginning, they will learn: (a) how successful people think, (b) successful ways to take rejection, and (c) view failure as a learning process.

Most people give up or choose the career of least resistance. Many come so close to success and never realize what they could become. However, Artis taught us how to overcome and not let negative responses prevent future success. Being exposed to Artis for six months is better than what you could gain at an Ivy League school. If new sales forces can just listen to him, your attitude and results will change in a positive way. There is nobody close to Artis Webb!

Kirby taught me how to think, change lives, and move from seventy-five dollars to independently wealthy. If you do not have the mental toughness, you will give up. However, as the saying goes, "winner never quits, and a quitter never wins!" The people that do not make it in Kirby are the people that quit. Within five years, they will move through five different jobs. However, they could have invested all five years and created success within one successful job like Kirby. Success is within you; success or failure, it is up to YOU! We could have Jesus come in and run motivational meetings, but when he leaves, it's up to you. "We all know what to do, but we DON'T do what we know." You will gain a wealth of knowledge, transform your life, and you will learn this in five days or less. There is no other job that will provide this type of outcome.

We motivated sales forces around the world.

—Salvatore Sorbera

Accepting the Kirby sales opportunity allowed us to travel to Australia, New Zealand, and Europe to motivate people in those countries. Interestingly, wherever one travels around the globe, we all have the same desires. Sorbera traveled to Indonesia where the average salary is $200 per month. He will never forget kids dressed up in shirts and ties for every sales meeting. Dealers supported this dress code even in one-hundred-degree weather. If these kids secured one sell in a month, they were in a greater position than the average person was. Regardless of their humble surroundings, they worked seven days a week. Most people would not continue investing thirty days seven days a week with an outcome average of two sales. However, these kids are happy and thankful! Although they live in chaos without televisions, they are happy for the Kirby opportunity!

Another unforgettable experience ensued in the Philippines. In the United States, sometimes we exhibit road rage, become impatient if someone cuts us off, or blow the horn to the hilt! However, people in the Philippines have polite drivers who engage each other. Artis does the same thing. He makes it a point to impact people's lives in a positive way. He takes people as though they were raw materials and turn them out, and when Artis is finished, people will result as a light turned on permanently. This is important, because a wealth of new sales folks arrive with negative influences or propaganda imposed by significant others or without positive reinforcement.

People want you to live their dream. I had to live MY dream!

—Salvatore Sorbera

Sorbera shared what friends or significant others will say, "Are you crazy selling vacuum cleaners?" You have to invest a wealth of personal sacrifice. People who are not willing to make sacrifices are influenced by loved ones and succumb to their influences. Sorbera shares, "If I listened to the people who told me I was crazy for doing what I am doing . . . *I wouldn't be* living a life of wealth in Hawaii now! People want you to live their dream. I had to live *my* dream! Therefore, I turned those people out. They only see what is good for them, not what's good for me." Thus, it is important to maximize patience, listen to the Webb-based science, and do not let anyone tell you what you cannot do. Listen to Artis instead of the typical status quo. Artis is an authentic giver who does not expect anything in return. This level of character is very different from the quid pro quo society. He gave me the gifts of inspiration,

knowledge, sharing of thought leadership, and value-added jewels important
for my development. I love that man! Artis will motivate people until the day he
dies; his influence is never-ending. *Thanks, Artis, for making a positive difference
in my life! —Sincerely, Salvatore Sorbera*

Dedicated to Dr. Dana Berry, former Kirby Dealer

Mr. Webb's leadership created a ripple effect.

—*Dr. Dana Berry*

Dr. Dana Berry is a successful dentist in California. While attending
college, he became a part-time dealer with the Kirby Company. Mr. Webb
provided Dr. Berry an opportunity that moved beyond the Kirby Company and
his life. He taught Berry to FIRST love himself. This is the second-greatest love
of all. If God made you, then you have a fighting chance! Mr. Webb invited Dr.
Berry into a completely new world. Prior to Kirby, Dr. Berry was considered a
manic-depressive. This mind-set was the product of a negative environment.
Such conditioning started in the fifth grade. Educational leaders told him he
was retarded. Because of this stigma, several professors said, "You're not college
material and therefore cannot learn." He entered a mental institute twice a
week and heard adults claim, "There's something wrong with you." However,
this diagnosis arrived because he refused to accept their beliefs. These beliefs
and environments became a cycle of failure and conferred failure based on
other perspectives. Dr. Berry recalled prior employment where he was promised
one thing, completed the work, and did not receive the endgame promised.
However, Mr. Webb arrived and interrupted the cycle of conditioned failure by
placing him on an upward path to success.

As a phenomenal coach, Mr. Webb empowered him to create success that
is not contingent upon his past, but his vision and hard work to move forward.
Thus, he organized a program to help him rise as a sales professional, and
the same program has helped him one thousand times more than expected.
A wealth of skills developed via Webb's daily professional development sales
clinics. For example, one course featured the subject of "Doors." When doors
close in our faces, these are just door of another opportunity; it is not personal!
Some may remember the game show that required you to pick a door. You
may also recall door no. 1, 2, or 3; one may be powerful and the other not so
powerful. The most important component was your attitude. When you select
that door, your positive or negative infection transferred to the customer.
Equipped with this positive attitude, Webb allowed Dr. Berry to work whenever
he wanted to work, earn as much capital he required, pay his college tuition,

and then go on and become the doctor desired. In order to reach this goal, he remained focused and consistent, and he produced fantastic results!

IF you look at the most successful companies, the individuals within that company who "represent success" often look alike. However, in the Kirby sales business, race, looks, diversity, and influence do not matter. Everyone receives the same resources to rise from an even playing field, of which delivered results. Some of the systems Mr. Webb taught included the ROL program. This step process enabled him to become an effective closer. Today, Dr. Berry applies the same approach in the dental business. He transfers that positive infection to his patients by explaining the importance of a smile and good attitude. Moreover, he inquires as to how they see their life, as a smile or a frown. Within any successful business, we are always selling. So Dr. Berry shares, "I don't have assistants, only customer service and sales associates. In addition, we leave all negativity in the parking lot outside. Our focus is to entertain, take care of the customer, and create rapport with customers." If you are stuck, we will walk you through it and teach you how to supersede the customer's expectations. Most dentist offices average three to four new patients per month. However, because of the ROL program, this enabled Dr. Berry to build a successful practice at an average rate of one hundred new customers or patients per month. That is fantastic!

Companies recruit executives based on their prior ability to sell. However, Mr. Webb told us, "We are more powerful than we know, more positive . . . regardless of where we came from. We can go out and make it happen!" Mr. Webb took us from nothing and taught us how to close, and we learned how to sell by starting with ourselves. One cannot be successful in the sales business if you are always conning or cheating people or selling a product that will leave them in a worse situation. Webb empowered our mind-set (where training starts) by coaching sales leaders to stand up in front of the team and receive recognition, positive reinforcement, authentic training, and strategies to fix whatever problem is hindering our success in business and life. This mind-set equipped Dr. Berry with a positive compass to navigate, create, and succeed at other opportunities in life. Webb does not realize the incredible impact he made on Dr. Berry's life. However, he was able to learn and complete this transformation in less than a year.

Today I give my customers every option available, including doing nothing. However, I also educate them regarding the consequences of doing nothing. Such as if you do not floss, you will lose many teeth. However, these tried and tested principles were learned by attending Webb's daily sales clinics. We learned how to sell ourselves first, because you could wake up with a negative attitude. However, by the time you departed from the sales meeting, you are pumped, committed, and positive. When your attitude is great, you are ready to take on the world with optimism. All these memories of the Webb-based science prepared me for one path: success! However, without an opportunity to work, you will not have anything worthwhile to pursue.

Dr. Berry arrived to the Kirby Company during a time when he was behind on his rent and maintained zero money for gas. However, if he could just pay for college through Kirby, it would result in the ultimate opportunity. Mr. Webb was no stranger to hard times. He was born in North Carolina and experienced challenges of hatred, but one cannot tell he endured this journey. He transcended that environment and represents the shining 2 percent of successful people in the nation. However, he is a legend because he provided an even playing field for future sales leaders to develop success. Mr. Webb's leadership created a ripple effect. For example, I arrived from Charlotte, North Carolina, born in the projects, and was told over thousands of times I could not make it. However, today I am a successful dentist with my own practice in California. In addition, I have two girls and a son. My nineteen-year-old daughter received a full scholarship to Notre Dame. Like my wife, her mom, she is also studying to become a physician. Added to this legacy is my fourteen-year-old son. As an eighth grader, he scored in the 99 percentile, received straight As and scholarships to attend high-performing high schools.

As mentioned, when you throw a stone in a pond, a ripple touches every corner of the lake. Mr. Webb's leadership's ripple effect has empowered thousands of people. For example, his inspiration and coaching enabled me to work with Serena and Venus Williams, the no. 1 professional tennis players, for over twenty-one years. I have engaged the no. 1 players in the world of tennis, who were also inspired by their father and outstanding coach. No one has accomplished the success achieved by Serena and Venus Williams, which I am proud to be a part of this journey.

> *You're more important than the CEO of the company! IF you don't make sales, the CEOs don't matter.*
>
> *—Artis Webb*

The outcomes arrive because I was inspired by the no. 1 coach in the world. Mr. Webb taught me the value of loving yourself, telling yourself you are great, and sticking to the work of the program. Once he sat down with Edward Caldwell and me. He invested an hour during this session, reviewing all the things that are positive and powerful about us. Further, he confirmed our assets to the company and to each other. Because we often come from such negative environments, we are inclined to go negative. Webb inspired his sales team to stand up-front, receive recognition, positive reinforcement, and strategies to fix the problem, thus providing a positive compass to navigate in life beyond the Kirby Company. How amazing when you consider Mr. Webb also arrived to the Kirby Company from a negative environment. No doubt he has witnessed sit-ins, friends, various challenges, etc. However, he was able to transcend all that negativity into a positive, confirming his own values. Mr. Webb taught us that once you know WHO you are, then little things could not stop you.

Sometimes we arrive with a negative belief about ourselves. However, he empowered us via context to underscore how important the salesperson is to society and the world's economy. Once he shared, "You're more important than the CEO of the company! IF you don't make sales, the CEOs don't matter." On another occasion, Mr. Webb observed the team moping around and complaining. Instead of telling us how we should feel or what we should do, he set the example as a leader and took us into the field. Upon arrival, he knocked onto a customer's home at 11:00 p.m. just to show us we can do this! That is a leader, a person who talks the talk and walks the walk.

I am the Artis Webb protégé . . . he gave me a FAIR advantage!

—*Dr. Dana Berry*

If you have never enjoyed a positive role model or sponsor in your family or circle, Mr. Webb provided the example of what African American role models should look like. Every day he gave me motivational CPR (communicated positive reinforcement). Mr. Webb looked like a professional, and despite his struggles, he never aired one negative word. His example in word and deed destroyed all the other negative stereotypes. Sometimes we do not know our power. Our value is not always communicated in the media. However, Dr. Berry learned about leadership and what a role model should look like by watching Mr. Webb. He always shifted the focus from our problems to our strengths and on what is positive. He changed our perspective on life! *I AM the Artis Webb protégé.* The world could learn from Artis Webb. He gave me a FAIR advantage. As he has inspired people in over seventy countries, I am hoping the ripple effect continues by allowing him to set up schools so he can continue to train us—people of all cultures and background on the local and global turf! *Thank you, Mr. Webb! You are my heart and passion. Thus, I send my love and respect! —Dr. Dana Berry*

Like Mr. Stewart, I share that satisfaction in reflecting on an accomplished sales career. Like my mom always said, believing in self means shedding all your doubts. Now I am happier than I had thought I'd be and anxious to watch the legacy of what sales leaders YOU will become and develop. At the TOP, you will see me! However, the reason I am here is to help you understand. You TOO can get what you want in life. You can "if you think you can!" (Henry Ford). Therefore, I leave my mother's final thoughts with you: "*The road to the top will always be rough. There is no easy way! Finally, the door of opportunity stands before you, and there will not be a single man or woman who will be able to stop you!"*

Because you can if you think you can. You will become what you think about most. Therefore, THINK positive, THINK big, ACT big, get BIG, and most of all, do all you can to become successful in this life! Remember, as Sal said, "Life gets better when you get better." All the best, and remember your best days are yet to come!

CHAPTER 11

What Is Next for the Head Rhino?

You cannot be financially successful until you
share success with others.

—*Artis Webb*

The United States Declaration of Independence maintains that all men are created equal, but there is a top 5 percent of the population that evolves to the level of Mr. Artis Webb. The evolution of Artis Webb was no accident. How did this transformation take place, which caused Artis to arise to a certain status that is considered higher than 95 percent of his fellow man? Believe me, it was not easy.

Early in his childhood, Artis began to sharpen the tools that he would need to become an outstanding salesperson and businessperson. As a youth working in the fields harvesting produce, his mother, Christine Webb, instilled in him discipline, endurance, and a competitive spirit. His first employers, Reverend James Moore and Mr. Robert Webb, trained him to follow instruction and to take pride in his work performance.

In school, Artis's teachers (Mrs. Azzelia Ferebee, Mrs. Dorothy J. Price, Mrs. Daisy Williams, and Mr. Peter W. Littlejohn) and superintendent S. D. O'Neal made him aware of his intellectual gift to comprehend concepts and to manipulate numbers and math problems. These teachers took a personal special interest in Artis. Living in a small rural community, the teachers knew that Artis's family life was dysfunctional and abusive. His personality and positive attitude served as magnets, and often these teachers invited Artis to live in their homes for short periods.

After finishing high school, Artis joined the United States Air Force. His military experience provided and exposed him to different nationalities and cultures, in addition to the importance of keeping his body physically fit in order to perform certain task. There was a period in Artis's life that he was introduced to many friends that sat in high places among their bookshelves. The various authors of these books strengthened his mind and intellectual fortitude, which enabled him to overcome many obstacles. Friends such as Willie Jolley, Dr. Spencer Johnson, Brian Tracy, Anthony Robbins, Andrew Matthew, Earl Nightingale, Zig Ziglar, Jim Rohn, Og Mandino, Scott Alexander, Les Brown and "Values of Quotes," and many others are the writers Artis emulated. These hundreds of friends through the years provided Artis with inspirations to stay on the path of success when other people threw in the towel. Artis Webb read these books so thoroughly and carefully that his life, his total being, was shaped according to their recommendations. Like many good teacher, he learned his subject matter so well that he was able to explain and share these principles to others that he started in the business.

The love, desire, and passion that Artis had for reading were ignited by two of the greatest motivational speakers and salespersons of all times. The innovators referred to were none other than Zig and his brother Judge Ziglar. In 1974, Artis's business suffered a devastation experience; it was burned to the ground. During that time, Dave Stewart was Artis Webb's distributor. Artis Webb was the top salesperson in Dave Stewart's business, and his organization flourished because of Artis's efforts. Dave valued Artis so much that Zig Ziglar wrote a book and alluded to Artis's (not by name) work habits and his skills in closing sales. Financially, Artis was very special to Dave Stewart. After the fire event, Mr. Stewart had the foresight to notice that his no. 1 salesperson, Artis, was having a hard time and going through a period of depression. Dave immediately called up an associate, Mr. Zig Ziglar, to spend time with Artis and to fix his broken spirit. It was this time spent with celebrity authors and motivational speakers Zig and Judge Ziglar that Artis developed the zeal for reading and the intestinal fortitude to overcome devastation. Artis has never forgotten those experiences, and they severed him well throughout his Kirby career.

Closing Words from Artis

In considering my exodus from the business, there are many individuals whom I trained and developed that will continue the philosophical mentoring, reinforcing their vision and innovative development of people. Their success fosters our program and leadership teachings. In addition, their examples serve as their validated success reflected in others. I pioneered the executive brand of Kirby as the first African American national sales manager and executive within the one hundred years of Kirby existence. In addition, I traveled to over seventy-plus countries as a goodwill ambassador. This great company allowed me to do the SAME THINGS, that's *s*timulate, *a*ctivate, *m*otivate, *e*ducate, *t*rain, *h*elp, *i*ncrease *n*ew *s*ales and *g*rowth around the globe. The company established me as the Head Rhino of Kirby because I shared the philosophy of Kirby and rhino charge throughout the world. Thus, my legacy in Kirby is documented by introducing the rhino charge philosophy throughout the world of Kirby to more than fifteen thousand men and women around the globe. The word *RHINO* stands for *r*iveted, *h*ungry, *i*ntense, *n*avigate, *o*ptimistic. Work through the negatives and maintain a new attitude at all times. Finally, stay organized and pursue the opportunity with positivity. There are many attributes that I would like to leave as a legacy. Always have a positive mental attitude (PMA), recruit and develop new salespeople and become successful entrepreneurs.

Go for the Green in 2014!

The final takeaway is dedicated to one of my greatest motivators, Zig Ziglar. He encouraged sales professionals to develop a personal mission statement to live by and develop successful behaviors. During the first thirty days, read three times per day. Rest in the morning and read at night, by yourself in front of a mirror. Stand upright, square your shoulders, look yourself in the eyes, quietly and firmly say in the first-person present tense. This will help you achieve the goal of green in 2014!

Your Personal Affirmation, Vision, and Mission Statement

I _____ AM a person of integrity with a good attitude and specific goals. I have a high energy level. I am enthusiastic, and I take pride in my appearance in what I do. I have a sense of humor, lots of faith, wisdom, vision, empathy, and courage to use my talents effectively. I have character, and I am knowledgeable. My convictions are strong, and I have a healthy self-image, a passion for what is right, and a solid hope for the future. I believe in continuous learning and being submissive to authorities. I possess good time management and use my time wisely.

I am honest, sincere, and hardworking person. I am tough but fair and sensitive; I am disciplined, motivated, and focused. I am a good listener, patient, and take decisive action. I am bold, authoritative, confident, and yet humble. I am an encourager, good finder, excellent communicator, and I am developing winning habits. I am a student, a teacher, a self-starter, and I am self-sufficient. I am obedient, responsible, dependable, and prompt. I have a servant's heart, ambitious, and a team player. I am personable, optimistic, and organized. I am consistent, considerate, and resourceful. I am intelligent, competent, persistent, and creative. I am health conscious, balanced, sober, and drug-free. I am flexible, punctual, and thrifty.

I AM an honorable person who is truly grateful for the opportunity life has given me. These are the qualities of a winner I was born to be, and I am fully committed to develop some marvelous qualities with which I have been entrusted. Tonight I am going to sleep wonderfully well. I will dream powerful, positive dreams. I will awaken energized, refreshed, and tomorrow is going to be a magnificent day. No matter what this day may bring, I will make it a SUCCESS. I know there are only two pains in life: the pain of regret and the pain of discipline. I will discipline myself to always be an active force in my life. Regardless of what it takes, I will always believe and succeed in reaching my sales goal today! For the rest I will remember my past circumstances do not equal my future progress. I _____ AGREE to read and commit to memory within the next thirty days.

Remember the Head Rhino Charge!

RHI, RHI, Rhino! RHINO, RHINO! DA DA DO DA DA DAAAA!

Positivity, Diversity, and Opportunity

It is critical for you to think GOOD things about yourself. According to one study, "Within groups of thirty or more people, 60 percent suffer from very low self-esteem because they compare themselves to others." Thus, they never achieve their full potential. However, that does not apply to you! Believe YOU deserve the best that life has to offer! I was fortunate to discover that Kirby *is* a people business. As I evolved around the business, the company was composed of different backgrounds from different places. Such unique differences increased my appreciation for people, understanding that diversity is about inclusion growth opportunities for everyone in business. The entire human race wants the same things: love and respect. We start expanding diversity and inclusion by giving people an opportunity to develop and grow. Ask yourself, what opportunity am I giving people in my company or community? This perspective moves us to expand product offerings beyond demographics of today. You may seek a single parent trying to put food on the table. Another group may reflect a part-timer or college student trying to finish without student loans. The situation varies from talent to talent or state to state. These people all want to have a better life. They want the same opportunity that we had. Continued success in Kirby is contingent upon our ability to mold people, to impart skills they need for success, and to value and develop diversity.

Therefore, the expression that perception is reality is not necessarily true because you can never capture the true essence of people until you get to know them as a person. In the '70s, this was the environment encountered when I started with Kirby. In addition, many people did not know about diversity. This group viewed different people as a threat to their lifestyle. Thus, initially Kirby did not think I was qualified to sell. However, I proved them wrong, just like so many others in the audience accomplished.

We arrived to this location by looking beyond our limited view of selves. The world's population is too diverse to impose our limitations on others. I challenge you to find people with explosive human potential that is ready to be tapped! They all come from different walks of life. You simply need to open your eyes and become more conscious of others—people who are blind do this naturally. A blind person cannot see. He or she does not judge people for what they are on the outside. Instead, they evaluate people for the character perceived on the inside. That is the location of your core value, desire, and beliefs.

Tell YOUR Story

Everyone has a story to share. When you first arrived to Kirby, you are similar to a blank sheet of paper. In time, you'll add more colorful experiences to your script. If you do not like your story, rewrite it! Share your story every day. The best thing about Kirby is that you can always start over. Moreover, you have a team cheering you on to success. Remember, I had to start over in the '70s when my office burned down because of a hate crime. This event resulted in a loss of financing and a $15,000 sales tax liability. The IRS said they would padlock my office within thirty days. My top choice was to return to the field and work. So I turned the situation around by immediately putting on 105 presentations, and I sold 105 cash sales in a row. I am so happy I pursued Kirby! This company provided a means to plan and support my family. In addition, I was honored to introduce the concept of diversity and a need to build understanding of others. This journey increased my knowledge and value of self and others.

Artis's Closing Words of Inspiration

When you do the common things in life in an uncommon way,
you will command the attention of the world.

—*George Washington Carver*

It is true that occasionally we don't recognize the greatness among us. However, I always valued the greatness in others. Moreover, I am cognizant that it is not how much wealth that one acquires but it is having a vision with standards, integrity, values, convictions, and the ability to affect those around me positively. The greatest legacy I will leave behind is that *IF* an ordinary individual like me maintains the passion and desire to succeed, the company provides the same program and diverse culture for your success. Within this literary work and various examples across the globe, people continue to arrive with a measure of success!

Always remember the inspiring words from my mentors Dave Stewart and Mr. Gene Windfeldt, Jimmy Iorio, Bud Miley, Sal Sorbera, Marshal Heron, Kevin Pertmier, and Dave Kayne: Here's one secret in life: you will not have many opportunities in the world to become successful! Make today count. Invest in the success of your team, apply the knowledge of your distributor, the company, and create your legacy as the sales leader and guru to come! Then most of all, remember, "Your best has not been recruited yet. As well as your best days are yet to come!"

While you are recruiting, building a successful business, investing time in family and spirituality, do not neglect doing the things that keep you inspired. For example, as a teenager, I loved to draw. One of my most important pictures was a drawing of a bulldog head. After finishing high school, I traveled with my Uncle Charles "Lindsay" Lindberg to New York. While working on a trash truck in New York, I drew cartoons. I deferred this inspirational hobby and possible career path as a cartoonist when I joined the US Air Force. However, I am going to find a sketchbook and factor some of these hobbies back into my life.

What Inspires the Head Rhino?

I am humbled when I read expressions from friends and former sales leaders who shared how this same level of commitment influenced them to become millionaires.

—Artis Webb

Maintaining an adaptable and growth-oriented mind-set helped me to evolve from poverty and a dysfunctional "bootleg" house frequented by heavy drinkers (and more) to arrival as a successful entrepreneur and leader. Sometimes we arrive to success *without* a sense of duty to give back. Along the journey, I never lost my strong sense of commitment to family and community. It was my privilege to purchase the same home my mother cleaned for living as a gift of appreciation for her hard work! How many men or women can claim this accomplishment for their mother? I enjoyed supporting college tuition for relatives. It was an honor to purchase school clothes so they could attend with a measure of pride and dignity. Most of all, I am humbled when I read expressions from friends and former dealers who shared how this same level of commitment *influenced a wealth of (non-blood related) individuals to become millionaires.*

These reflections and outcomes inspire me. My hope is for these examples to inspire you as a sales professional to "NEVER, NEVER, NEVER give up!" (Winston Churchill). This positive effect did not stop with my family. I continued to disseminate this positive attitude and way of life to thousands of people throughout the world. At times, I traveled for over 140 days, maintained as much jet lag as a comet, and earned enough frequent-flyer miles to go to the moon. A motivation to impart kindness, warmth, and motivation inspired my deliveries. Childhood conditions mandate that I continue to help others. With that conviction so strongly engraved in my total being, my life's prime directive will be geared toward helping my fellowman—whether my next step evolves into the community, a nonprofit, consultant, motivational speaker, or other path. Stay Tuned! In the meantime, I will depart with one final appeal.

We live in a world that consists of bums, criminals, and thugs.
We are constantly bombarded with violence, crime, and drugs.
If you plan to live a quality life with a lot of class,

> *It is the person who refrains from those barbiturates that will*
> *truly last.*
> *So stay in Kirby and learn the wisdom from the pros.*
> *It is a sure guarantee if your ultimate goal is to grow.*
> *Do not worry about the ups, downs, fears, and doubts.*
> *The nature of our business develops millionaires of people like*
> *you with clout!*

Go out and become committed, regimented, aspiring, zesty, and invest years doing something remarkable with your life!

Stay positive and passionate! Sincerely, Artis Webb

The End

INDEX

U

uncertainties, 27, 42, 145

W

Walker, Daryl, 85–89
watchers, 81, 83
Webb, Aaron, 43, 62–65
Webb, A. J., 20, 43, 61, 64, 67, 120–21
Webb, Christine, 9, 34–35, 39, 46,
    48–51, 69, 102, 166
Webb, Jack, 40
Webb, Julius, 36–40

Webb, Lindsey, 9, 38
Webb, Mehgan, 20, 43, 58–61, 64
Webb, Robert, 34–35, 166
Webb, Tonie, 9, 69–71
Windfeldt, Gene, 3–5, 9, 61, 105, 174
Wisinger, Bobby, 151–53
wonderers, 81, 83

Z

zeal, 18, 168
Ziglar, Zig, 71, 82, 167–69

CPSIA information can be obtained at www.ICGtesting.com
Printed in the USA
LVOW07*0004151014

408787LV00005B/68/P